# Bear's Forever

## Infernal Sons MC #1

## Carol Dawn

# Bear's Forever



Published by Carolyn Jacobs
Cover by Carolyn Jacobs

# Dedication

For those who think you can't.
You can.

# Blurb

Her

Twenty-five years in captivity, never once seeing the world outside the yard of my captors` home. My chance at escape has finally shown its head. Risking my life, I run. I run into an unknown world of tall buildings, fast-moving vehicles, loud noises, and big, scary, biker riding men.

I'M FREE...or so I thought.

The life I ran from is quickly catching up. I'm being hunted by the man who thinks he owns me and wants me back. But I feel safe because I'm protected by the man who wants my heart.

But what if that man is threatened by my past? Will I go back to a life of pain and captivity to save the man who truly owns me, heart and soul? Or, will I let him risk it all to protect me?

Him

As president of the Infernal Sons MC, everything I do is for my club; my brothers. That is, until the night a tiny, beautiful, shoeless woman runs into my life...literally.

The little slip of a woman turns my life upside down. Someone is after her and I will do everything in my power to keep her safe. Because SHE IS MINE, and no one will ever touch her again.

This woman could be the glue that holds my puzzled soul together. But, if I'm not careful, she could easily be the one who tears it apart.

*****WARNING*****

Intended for readers 18 and older. This book is highly radioactive due to the amount of "F-Bombs" these guys drop. Inside you will find violence, abuse and an adult situation or two. So, slip on that hazmat suit and proceed with caution.

*****HEALTH WARNING*****

This book is packed full of alpha male deliciousness, insta-something and enough over-sweetened romance that cavities are a real possibility. Keep your dentist on speed dial.

# PROLOGUE
## *Brian Pierce*

"Please, Brian. It feels like my insides are on fire. Just enough for one more. Please."

Sandra Brown stands in front of me begging for more money. Same story, different day. My once best friend, the mother of my offspring, is nothing more than a drug whore. Not that she was ever much of anything to begin with.

Pathetic woman.

"You keep expecting me to pay for your habit when I get nothing in return. Tell me, Sandra, what will you give me if I help you out?"

"What do you want?" she asks with a shaky voice.

I laugh as I walk toward her. "You know what I want. What I truly want. Give it to me and I will give you all the cash in my wallet."

Sandra stands motionless for a few moments before her eyes go wide.

"Can't I do anything else? Give you anything else apart from that?" she begs.

Shaking my head, I answer, "I have no other wish of you."

A moment's hesitation before a whispered, "Okay, I'll do it. I'll sign the papers."

Celebrating the victory internally, I walk to my office and grab the papers waiting on my desk. I walk back out to where Sandra is standing near the front door, hand her the papers and a pen, then show her where to sign.

A small hesitation, two, three, then she signs her name. Grabbing the papers, I turn to put them safely in my office. My assistant can have all the legal work started first thing in the morning.

Once I'm standing in front of Sandra again, I reach into my back pocket and grab my wallet. I take out every bill, around a grand or two, and shove it into her hands.

"I don't want to see you again, Sandra. Signing over all your parental rights of our child was the right choice, but you are no longer part of her life. Have I made myself clear?"

She nods.

"Good. Goodbye."

I open the door and usher her out. The moment both of her feet pass the threshold, I slam the door and walk over to the child.

"We have plans, you and me. You will make your father a very rich and powerful man one day. But first, we need to get you prepared. What do you say, child? You ready to make a deal with the devil?"

"Gah gub ba"

"Oh, I'm not the devil, girl. He's but five years old. One day, you will look him in the eyes and take him as your husband."

My plans have finally begun. In twenty-five years', time, I will be in such a place of power that nothing and no one can stop me.

# Chapter One
## *(Twenty-Five Years later)*

I hear him running behind me. The stomping of his boots getting louder by the second. I don't know how much longer I can keep going. I'm so tired. I just want to lay down, close my eyes and let fate take over. But I worked so hard to get this far. I'm not giving up now. Ignoring the pain in my body and the tightness in my chest, I continue running.

There are no lights on in the surrounding buildings and I have yet to see a single car drive by. This was a poor time to attempt my escape.

"Oh girl, I'm getting tired of this game of yours."

Hearing his voice, I almost pass out with fear. I can't let him catch me. If he does, then the last twenty-five years will be child's play compared to what he will do. Digging deep down I find a small boost of energy. I speed up and run down the street with everything that I have. The sky is moonless tonight. The sun set hours ago, and the darkness is so deep that if it wasn't for the streetlights, I wouldn't be able to see my own hands. So, the decision to run down the even darker ally I see up ahead seems like a stupid choice, but maybe I can find a place to hide and catch my breath.

Coming to the head of the ally, I turn hoping he didn't see which way I went. My heart is instantly filled with dread when I notice the ally I stupidly decided to run down was a dead end. Seeing a dumpster at the end of the ally, I fling myself between the dumpster and the back wall. Pulling my knees up to my chest and wrapping my arms around my legs, I try to catch my breath as quietly as I can.

I don't know what to do. If I try to run from this ally, he will see me, and there is simply no way to escape him from back here. If I just sit here, he will eventually find me. My tears silently fall when I realize that no matter what choice I make I will be going back to my prison. Laying my forehead on my knees, I cry for my lost childhood. I cry for my hopeless future.

That's when I hear it. The low rumble of deep voices. I look up and notice, for the first time, a door directly across from where I sat. My hope flickers back to life as I jump up and dash across the ally. I grab the handle and push my way inside as fast as I can. Once inside I instantly turn to shut the door quietly.

The first thing that registers is how warm it is. I have on no shoes and just a small, thin nightgown. It's October in Ohio, and the nights tend to get very cold. My whole body is shivering and each goosebump I have feels like the prick of a needle. So, the warmth of the building was a wonderful gift. The second thing I notice was that the voices I heard from outside have stopped.

With my eyes to the floor, I slowly turn around. I can feel there are several people in the same room that I'm standing it without looking up. Taking a deep breath, I raise my eyes and freeze.

"Oh...my," I whisper under my breath.

Standing around a large table staring right at me are about six very large, very scary-looking men. Each man has a look of absolute anger on his face. I'm frozen in place, too afraid to move or say anything, and too afraid to turn back. Some chairs are pushed back, and some are sideways on the floor like the men stood up too fast and knocked them over. The man standing at the head of the table has the most terrifying yet beautiful face I have ever seen. Not that I've seen many faces in my life but even those I have seen in person or on television don't compare to the man staring holes into my soul.

"No place to go now, girl," I hear *his* muffled voice say from right outside the door.

At the sound of *his* angry voice, all the men turn their eyes from me to the door.

Decision made, I run to the handsome, scary faced man at the head of the table and hide behind him. The fear I felt toward him moments ago has lessened, and my only thought is, 'please don't let *him* find me'. I push my shivering body flat against the man's back and tightly grip the black leather vest he's wearing.

He's so tall that the top of my five-foot-one body stops well below his shoulders. The man doesn't react to me invading his space. None of the men I walked in on say a single word as I cower behind this person hoping he will be my barrier against the evil about to walk through the door.

Hearing a loud bang, I can only assume that the door has been forcibly pushed open and slammed against the wall. I feel the man I'm hiding behind stiffen and that frightens me. I press my head against his back and try to slow my heartbeat for fear *he* will hear it. Please, God, I can't go back.

I have no reason to believe this group of men will protect me, but this is my only choice. I just hope and pray I haven't made a mistake.

"Where is she?"

I can feel my panic rising at the sound of *his* voice being so close. I tremble and this time it isn't from the cold. I can hear my breathing getting louder, and I know any second *he* will find me. Suddenly a strange warmth runs up my side and I instantly relax. Looking down, I see the man has reached back and wrapped his large hand around my left hip. What a strangely gentle gesture for such a large scary man.

"Who the fuck are you?" I hear. I know it's the man in front of me because I feel his back vibrate as he speaks. His voice is so low that the sound comes out more like a growl than a human voice.

"Oh, I... I'm looking for someone," *he* stutters.

"A young woman, real short and curvy with super light blonde hair down to her bottom, big brown eyes, She's in her nightshirt and nothing else. She must be cold. Probably scared out of her mind. She's not used to so many buildings. I'm really worried about her. Have you gentlemen by any chance seen her around?"

The room is so quiet you could hear a pin drop. Then a few men start laughing.

"Did you just call us gentlemen?" one man asks.

The man in front of me chuckles.

"Ink, show this...gentleman where the door is then throw his ass out of it," he says.

"Now you listen here you heathen..."

The man I'm cowering behind releases my hip and rushes forward. Before I can even get a small glimpse around his back there are two new men, wearing identical black leather vests as the first one, now standing in front of me. It happened so fast there is no way my captor saw me.

"I don't know who you think you are but let me tell you a little something about me," the man's voice has somehow dropped even lower than before as he continues to speak. “My name is Bear, and I am the mother fucking president of the Infernal Sons, MC. You just barged in on a very important meeting I was having with my brothers. In the middle of the night. You have two options. Turn around and leave or I'll introduce you to Trigger. If you choose option two, then option one will no longer be viable because you'll have a hole between your eyes. I'll give you one minute to make your choice.”

I hear a thump and someone gasping for air.

“Please, I need to find her. She's never been out on her own before.”

“Thirty seconds,” the man I now know is Bear says.

“Okay, I'm leaving. If you see her, call me. It's not safe for her to be out here on her own. I'll leave my card on the table.”

I can hear him walking closer. Most likely to do what he says and drop his card on the table. The closer he gets the faster my heart beats and the shorter my breaths become. I'm about to pass out. I can feel it. I hear muffled voices, but it's drowned out by a high-pitched tone and the darkening of the room.

There’s a small bit of pressure on both sides of my face, and I hear a calm soothing voice calling for my attention. Eventually, the high-pitched noise vanishes and the world around me reappears. Bear is holding my face in his hands, and he's talking. I'm still not here enough to understand what he's saying but he does look a little worried. I wonder what caused him to worry.

Finally, I can hear his voice.

“Sweetheart, can you hear me?” Bear asks.

Not sure if I'm able to speak at the moment I nod my head.

“Good. That's good,” he says. “What's your name?”

Of all the questions in the entire world he could have asked me, why did it have to be that one? Why did it have to be the one question that breaks my heart open every time I think about it? My eyes water and the tears fall. I try to look down but Bears big hands are still wrapped around my face and he doesn't let me.

"Your name, what do I call you?"

Taking a deep breath, I answer the best I can with this lump in my throat. "Nothing."

Bear's eyes go dark and I can see how hard he's trying to remain calm.

"You are not nothing," he tells me. "But I really would like to know your name. Just your first name is fine."

He doesn't understand. I swallow the discomfort and try to explain my answer better.

"I..," my throat hurts. I try again. "I am... I have no birth name. I am called, girl."

Bear releases my face and starts pacing back and forth. I don't understand why he's so aggravated. I run to the corner of the room and make myself as small as I can while I cower in fear. When *he* became angry it never ended well for me. I watch as Bear calms himself and his eyes roam the room. Spotting me in the corner, his face softens a small bit, and he walks over to crouch in front of me.

"We'll get back to that," he says. "The man who chased you in here, who was he?"

I look up into the stormy blue eyes of Bear, and I answer him with the name of one of the two people I fear most in the whole world. The person who will stop at nothing to find me and take me back. The person who has held me captive for my whole life. Both of my cheeks are wet with tears when I take a breath and give Bear his answer.

"My father."

# Chapter Two
*Bear*

"Why exactly did we meet here instead of the clubhouse?" I ask.

"We have a rat."

I close my eyes and run a hand down my face. Just what I need. My Vice-President, Chains, called me about an hour ago and said we needed to call church immediately. But, somewhere besides the clubhouse. So, here we are, well past midnight, the other club officers, and me, all sitting around the table at Lucky. Lucky is the local bar run and owned by the Infernal Sons. We had to shut down tonight to install a new security system.

After Chains is finished speaking the room goes deathly silent. I open my eyes and see five sets of eyes looking back at me.

"Well...what do you have?" I ask.

"I got a call from an old buddy earlier from Columbus. He says he overheard some guys talking about the Infernal Sons." Chains pauses. "Prez, my buddy told me the exact plans for the Hernandez run we have scheduled two weeks from now."

Fuck.

"How the fuck is that possible? There is a total of six people who know those plans."

"That's why I wanted to meet here. I don't think for a second a single person in this room would turn rat," Chains says, confidently.

I agree with him. I don't think any brother here would betray the club. That only means one thing.

"Someone was listening. The walls in our meeting room are soundproof. Once the door is shut not a single sound can be heard from either side of it. No one overheard our plans during church" I said. "The clubhouse has bugs."

Just then the back door to the bar is shoved open and we all jump to our feet, chairs falling behind us. Before anyone can react, in runs a small female. She turns around so fast I don't get a look at her face, and she shuts the door much quieter than when she opened it. She just stands with her hand on the door handle for a few seconds before she turns around.

The second she looks up and I see her face I know my life is about to be turned upside down. She is the most beautiful person I have ever seen. Her hair is the lightest of blonde and her eyes are so dark they're almost black. She's a short beauty with curves that can make a man's mouth water. The only thing covering her smooth pale skin is a thin layer of fabric that stops just above her knees.

I'm about to say something when I hear a man's voice yelling from outside. The woman's eyes grow wide with fear. My protective instinct rushes forward and I step toward her but stop when I see her running right for me. She runs until she is slightly behind me and the little slip of a woman plasters herself right against my back. Not even a second later the same door she came through is shoved open, with much more force, and bounces against the wall.

A man is standing just inside the door. His eyes look wild. His arms are hung at his side and in one hand he is holding what looks to be a taser gun that most police officers use. I'm instantly on guard.

"Where is she?" crazy eyes asks.

I feel the woman at my back shake and her breathing is getting choppy. Reaching back, I touch whatever part of her body my hand reaches first. I feel the softness of her clothes, so I know about where I'm holding her. My hands are rough and calloused, but she doesn't seem to mind, and her breathing starts to even out.

"Who the fuck are you?" I ask, ignoring his question.

"Oh, I... I'm looking for someone." Crazy eyes keeps scanning the room hardly giving the brothers a glance. He explains what the someone he's looking for looks like. Sounds just like my little back warmer.

"Have you gentlemen by any chance seen her around?"

Ink, Brick, and Chains are laughing at crazy eyes calling us gentlemen. There isn't a single thing gentle about any of my brothers. I laugh with the thought of a gentle Trigger. That man has less emotion than a Jellyfish and reacts on instinct alone.

"Ink, show this.... gentleman where the door is, then throw his ass out of it," I say.

"Now you listen here you heathen..."

With a quick glance at Hawk and Brick, the two closest brothers, I rush forward trusting my men to have understood and protect the woman. I grab crazy eyes around the throat and squeeze just enough to make him struggle for his next breath, but not pass out before I want him to. I tell the man who I am, hoping he will recognize either my name or the clubs name.

I can tell when it dawns on him and his face turns white. I release his throat and after more rambling, he drops a card on the table and then walks out the door.

Standing there for a few minutes, I wait to make sure he doesn't come back. Once I'm satisfied, I turn and head back to the woman hidden behind Brick and Hawk. They move aside, and I rush forward. Her skin is pale and wet with sweat, she's shaking, and her eyes are glazed over. I know a panic attack when I see one. I cup her small, delicate face in my hands, trying to get her to focus on only one thing while I try and talk her out of her panic.

"Hey, sweetheart," I say softly. "He's gone now. It's okay. You're safe. No one is going to hurt you, I promise."

The color on her face comes back and her eyes are trying to focus. She's coming out of it. Thank fuck.

"Sweetheart, can you hear me?" I say.

She nods her head and I take a relieved breath. I don't know why the woman is having this effect on me. I'm not sure if I like it or not.

"Good. That's good. What's your name?" I ask.

The look in her eyes breaks my heart. She looks so defeated. My hands are still holding her when she tries looking away. I'm having none of that and keep her face right where I can see every single inch of it.

"Your name, what do I call you?" I ask softly.

"Nothing," she says with a voice so sweet.

Registering what she says I get pissed at crazy eyes all over again. I don't know what that man has done to this beautiful woman to make her think she is nothing, but I will stop at nothing to make sure he pays. Painfully. Slowly. I don't want her to have another panic attack, so I try to calm myself before speaking.

"You are not nothing," I say. "But I really would like to know your name. Just your first name is fine."

I don't like thinking of her as *the woman.* All I want is a name to call this beautiful person. I want to see if her name tastes as sweet as she looks.

Clearing her throat, she tells me, “I... I have no birth name. I am called, girl.”

The anger comes out in full force. I release her face gently and walk away, trying to remain calm so I don't scare her. She doesn't have a fucking name? They call her girl? Taking a deep breath, I turn around. She's not where I left her. Trying not to panic I quickly search the room and find her in the corner behind the table.

She looks so innocent and lost. I can't help but want to wrap her in my arms and hide her away from anyone who would harm her. I walk to her and crouch down so she doesn't have to move.

“We'll get back to that,” I tell her. “The man who chased you in here, who was he?”

The brownest eyes I have ever seen looks straight at me and shocks me for the fourth time in thirty minutes.

“My father,” she whispers, as the tears trail down her face and fall to the floor.

Her fucking father?

Until this moment my brothers have kept to the side quietly and allowed me to handle the woman without interfering. The moment she gave me her answer there was a whole eruption of pissed off men.

Feeling someone squeeze my shoulder I look back. Hawk, my blood brother, was standing there with a question in his eyes. Nodding that I understood, I turn back to the beauty with a small smile.

“Okay, baby, I need to talk to my brothers. You're safe here. No one will hurt you. Do you want to sit at the table for a bit?

She nods her head. I hold out my hand and wait patiently to see if she will accept. She slowly places her small, cold hand into mine and I help her up and walk her to the table.

"I'll be just a minute. I'm not leaving the room only heading over by the bar. Just wait here for me, okay?" I tell her.

She says nothing but again nods her head. I lightly squeeze the hand that was still tucked safely in my own and reluctantly let it go.

"What the actual fuck?" Hawk says when I make it over to the bar.

"I think I know him." Chains says. "Her father, I'm pretty sure I've seen him somewhere. I'll look into it and see if I can figure it out."

Rubbing my head, I address my VP. "Chains, see if Laura has any girl shit she can send over. Soaps, clothes, shoes. Whatever she cares to part with."

"Prez, none of my sisters' clothes will fit that tiny woman," Chains says.

"It's fine if they don't fit. Just as long as they cover her skin enough to keep her warm. And If you figure out who that bastard is, let me know."

One nod and I know I can count on Chains to take care of it.

"Hawk, how do you feel about debugging the club-house?" I ask.

"I'm on it, Prez. I'll send any pieces I find over to Slim and see if he's able to tell us anything."

Slim is a prospect and our clubs' electronic junkie. The man can hack into any system you put in front of him.

"Alright, church tomorrow at noon, my house. No more club business at the clubhouse until Hawk gives the word," I say.

"What about our new girl?" Trigger asks.

Glaring at the emotionless ass hat I say, "She isn't *our* new anything. She's off-limits. I see a single finger touching her and I'll break the owner's fucking arm. Are we clear?"

I get a unanimous *yes Prez.*

"I'm taking her back to my house. Hopefully, I can get some answers," I say.

With nothing more to say I turn and head back to the woman. Damn, she needs a fucking name.

"Come on, baby, I'm taking you home," I say as I reach for her hand.

Before I can reach her, she falls out of her chair and cries.

"No, p..p..please don't take me back there. I'll be g...good. I won't make a s…sound. Please," she begs.

I just stand there frozen with my hand still reaching for her. Then I realize what I said. She took it to mean I was taking her back to her father. I don't think so. If I have anything to do with it, she will never set those perfect eyes on that bastard again.

"Oh, no sweetheart," I tell her softly. "I will never take you back there. I was talking about my home. You can stay there in my guest room. No harm will come to you under my roof. We'll figure everything else out later. Do you trust me?"

I panic after a few seconds of her not saying anything. Then she gives me a small nod and places her hand in mine. Helping her up off the floor I gently pull her into my arms. Wrapping my arms securely around her I just hold her for a few minutes before I pull back.

Her hand still in mine, we walk toward the front of the building and out the door.

"Let's go home," I tell her. With those three words, another piece of my broken puzzle slides into place. This woman could be the glue that holds my puzzled soul together. But, if I'm not careful, she could easily be the one who tears it apart.

# Chapter Three

The moment we step outside I'm hit with an intense blast of cold. When I escaped my father's house earlier, I did it with only the clothes on my back. The chance I had been waiting for had finally happened and I couldn't risk my only opportunity by changing my clothes or even slipping on my shoes. So, I'm standing in the cold wearing only a thin nightgown with very little shoulder straps.

I shiver but don't complain about the cold for fear that Bear will see me as a spoiled child and change his mind about helping me. Regardless of my attempts, he must have noticed because he stops walking and pulls me against his body.

"Fuck, you're freezing," he says quietly before turning his head to look at the group of men exiting the bar behind us.

"Hawk, did you bring your truck?" Bear asks one of the men.

"Yep, it's parked out back."

I look up at the man Bear called Hawk and do a double-take. Hawk is the spitting image of Bear. Brothers. Twins. They both have the same long thick beards, a good head of thick hair and eyes so blue I could practically see my reflection. Not to mention they both could be mistaken for giants. At the least, well over six feet tall and wide enough that two of me could stand side by side behind one of them and still be completely hidden.

Although they are identical twins, I can easily tell the two apart. Hawk's voice isn't quite as low toned as Bears and while Bear seems broody and fierce, Hawk is all smiles and relaxed. Also, Hawk's hair is black, where Bear's is dark brown.

"I need you to follow me on my bike," Bear says to Hawk while rubbing his hands up and down my arms. "She's not dressed for a joy ride tonight."

One side of Hawks mouth tips up to a soft grin and he nods. He throws Bear a set of keys and walks away. We start walking again and Bear is leading me where he wants me to go with his hand pressed against the small of my back. I'm so focused on the warmth of his hand that I don't notice when we stop beside a massively big truck.

"Hop up sweetheart," he tells me.

I'm trying to think of a way to *hop up* without embarrassing myself. The truck is high up off the ground and I'm...well, I'm not. Hearing a chuckle, I turn around to see Bear's eyes are alive with humor. I feel my face heating up with the embarrassment I was trying to avoid.

Heck with it.

I turn toward the truck and take a step forward when suddenly I'm lifted and placed gently in the passenger seat. My back barely hits the seat and I try to hide the wince of massive pain I felt from the small contact. Bear grabs the seat belt, pulls it across my body and leans over me to buckle it in. Before he backs away, he lifts his hand and slides his thumb softly down my cheek. So softly it tickles. When he finally backs up and shuts the door, I let out the breath of air I didn't even realize I was holding.

Seconds later he's sitting beside me and starting the truck.

"Let's get the heat going and get you warmed up," he says as he messes with some buttons on the dash in front of us.

Feeling a blast of heat hit me I instantly relax in the

seat and close my eyes. Gosh, that feels so good. We start moving and my eyes dart open to look around. The only time I've ever seen the outside world was during my escape and I wasn't paying much attention to what was around me. I've never seen so many buildings. Or vehicles. Or trees. Everything was going by so fast and I was starting to feel sick. I close my eyes and allow the darkness to sooth me from so much unknown.

"Hey, you alright?"

I sigh because I know I can't lie to him and the truth will only bring out more questions I'm not yet prepared to answer. I ready myself for the task I know will come.

"I'm fine, thank you. I've just never been in a vehicle before and my vision isn't used to things moving so fast. Do you mind if I just close my eyes until we arrive at your home?" I ask him.

I see a tick in his jaw, but he answers with a simple "of course" and says nothing more. I'm shocked that he didn't ask me all the questions I could see he truly wanted to know.

I must have spoken my thoughts out loud because he says, "Oh, I'll be getting answers to my questions, baby. I just want you warm and rested before we even begin."

I nod my head and close my eyes. I must have drifted off to sleep because the next thing I know everything goes silent and we're no longer moving.

"Wake up sleeping beauty, we're home."

When I open my eyes, I see a single light illuminating the front porch of a log cabin. It's too dark to notice any detail other than the hanging swing and chairs sitting on the porch. I look around and notice a light illuminating another porch not too far away from Bear's home. Apart from the two homes, and probably many creatures surrounding the woods, there is nothing else out here.

I keep telling myself that I should be scared. I don't know this man and I let him drive me out in the middle of nowhere. I don't know his intentions. I know he's a very dangerous man. A simple look into his eyes could tell you that. But I honestly believe, with everything that I am, this man will do me no harm.

I know evil. I've looked it straight in the eyes. I've tried to love it. I've tried to comfort it. The man currently opening my door with a smile on his face is not evil. He may make himself appear hard and mean to others and is most definitely capable of inflicting harm, but he is not evil. Not even close.

"You ready to go inside?" Bear asks me.

I give him a small smile for the first time. "Is this really your home?" I ask instead of answering his question.

The truth is, I'm scared. I don't think he would hurt me but I'm afraid of being locked inside a room again.

"It sure is," he says with a voice so proud. "And, that cabin over there is my blood brothers. Hawk."

"Blood brothers?" I ask. I knew Hawk was his brother, but I didn't understand why he termed it, *blood brother.*

"We're part of a motorcycle club," I hear Hawk say as he stops to stand right beside Bear. "The men back at the bar are also members."

"It's not just a club; it's a family. We're all brothers." Bear says. "Hawk is the only brother that is of blood and not just choice."

I nod my head that I understood. Turning so my legs are hanging out of the truck I brace myself for the jump to get down. Once again, I feel myself being lifted. This time I'm carried toward the house, bridal style. My face is turning red and I try to tell him that I'm capable of walking, but he beats me to it.

"It's freezing out here sweetheart, I don't want your feet to touch the cold ground when I can just as easily, and quickly, carry you inside."

The next thing I know Hawk is opening the cabin door for Bear and we walk into a beautiful living room. The outside of the cabin seems so rustic. The inside is the complete opposite. Hanging from the wall is a very large flat-screen television. The couch that sits opposite the tv is solid black. As well as the coffee table and the side tables on either side of the couch. The cabin is surprisingly tidy for a man's home and you can definitely tell a man lives here. It's just begging for a woman's touch.

Instead of putting me down Bear walks me past the living room and down a hallway. He stops in front of a door and then gently places my feet on the floor.

"This is the bathroom," he says pointing at the door in front of us. "Directly across from the bathroom is the guest room. Why don't you take a hot bath while I get your room ready for you?"

I look at the floor trying to muster up some courage. He doesn't know this but talking is hard for me. Not painful hard, just hard in general. I was never allowed to talk much. If I did so without being asked a direct question I would be punished. Painfully.

"Thank you," I whisper. "Thank you so much for helping me. I promise to be good."

He reaches his hand up and with one finger guides my face until I'm looking in his eyes. With a frown on his face, he says, "You're welcome. I won't let any harm come to you and we'll talk about what you need protecting from, tomorrow. For now, go relax in the tub. Take your time, sweetheart. I'll have soup and a warm bed ready for you when you get out."

With a small nod, I turn and go into the bathroom but stop when Bear says something.

"One more thing, we need a name for you. Is there any name you want to have?" He asks me.

Shaking my head, I whisper, "No, I've always wanted a name, but I wanted someone to pick it for me. It doesn't mean as much if I choose one myself." I blush knowing that what I've said sounds silly. Who wouldn't want to pick their own name? I just feel that a name I choose myself has no meaning like the ones most parents or loved one pick for a newborn child.

"Okay," he says with a smile. "How about Rose?"

I tilt my head to the side wondering why he would choose that name. It's a beautiful name. Do I deserve such a beautiful name?

"Why Rose?" I ask quietly.

With a smile, he says, "Because you blush so beautifully. Like a beautiful Rose."

Feeling myself blush at his silly compliment, I give him a small smile.

"Rose," I say as my smile widens and I blush deeper. "I love it. Thank you."

"I'll see you after your bath, sweet, beautiful Rose," he says.

Turning quickly so he can't see my annoying blush, I walk into the bathroom shutting the door behind me. I turn on the tub and while it fills, I remove my dirty gown trying to keep my painful cries silent. I just know it's really bad this time.

I turn to get a look in the mirror and cry at what I see. My father let him do this. He stood there and watched. Unlike the times my father had done so, this man pushed harder which means it will take longer to heal and will leave an even uglier scar.

I turn from the mirror and sink into the tub. Pushing my knees up I wrap my arms around my legs, lay my head on top of my knees and pray that the water will disguise my tears.

Bear is wrong.

I will never be a beautiful Rose. I will only ever be an ugly, damaged nobody.

# Chapter Four

*Bear*

I go to my chest of drawers and look for a shirt for Rose to wear until we can get her some clothes. Rose. A beautiful name for a beautiful woman. When she said that she wanted someone to give her a name, I couldn't think of anything more perfect. Every time she blushes her pale skin reddens all the way down her neck. I just wonder how far down her blush will actually go.

I'm heading back to the bathroom to put the clothes on the sink when I spot my twin leaning against the hallway wall with a knowing grin on his face.

"What's with the face?" I ask him.

His grin gets wider and he asks, "What's with the whistling?"

Ignoring his question, I walk away with his laughter following me. I was not whistling. Was I? Dammit. Okay, so maybe I was. I can't explain it. I feel relaxed having Rose in my home. I know we still have a ton to talk about, but I feel... happy.

Until I open the bathroom door.

Rose is sitting in the tub making herself as small as she can. Her head is resting on her knees and from the movement of her shoulders, I could tell she's crying. But that isn't what had my feet frozen to the floor.

On her back were dozens of scars. Both old and new. The newest scars couldn't have been more than a day old. Some even had drops of blood seeping out. A few were inflamed showing signs of an oncoming infection. I went from happy to fucking pissed instantly.

Knowing I will get all my questions answered soon I try to shove away the anger. I don't want to scare my beautiful Rose any more than she already is. Taking a deep breath, I walk the rest of the way into the bathroom.

"Rose, sweetheart, I have you a shirt and a pair of my boxers. The shirt will swallow you, but you can roll the boxers, so they won't fall off," I talk softly. She's still silently crying, and I don't know how to help her.

Normally I would just barge over there and take her into my arms, but I have a feeling that it would have the opposite effect of what I want. I slowly walk over and kneel beside the tub. I say nothing. I just want her to know that I'm here. I'm not sure how long I knelt there silently before her small voice filled the room.

"Bear," she whispers.

"Right here, baby"

Hearing her sniff and seeing the tears running down her face makes me want to kill someone. Preferably the someone who scarred her skin.

"I'm so frightened," she tells me. Her face is still laying on her legs, but her eyes are looking my way. Not looking in my eyes but at least they are pointed in my direction and not on the floor.

"Will you tell me why you're afraid?" I softly ask.

She stays silent for a few minutes before answering.

"I'm afraid he will find me."

"Your father?" I push.

"No," she says. I'm very confused. Her father was the one who chased after her a couple of hours ago and she was terrified of him. There is someone else out there who she fears even more?

"Who is *he,* Rose?"

"I also fear how easily I'm trusting you. I'm afraid that my instinct is wrong and you're not a good man. I'm ignorant of the real world. Of real people. I have no idea what to do. I'm so lost."

Hearing that she's afraid of me almost breaks me. "I swear to you, sweet girl, I will never cause you any harm. I can't explain why, because I don't understand it myself, but I have a feeling that my future depends on you." Her eyes flick up to meet mine. "Now, who is *he?*"

"May I please finish my bath and then I promise I will tell you everything you want to know?" she says.

"Including how you got those scars on your back?" I ask her.

She gives me a small nod, and I stand up and leave to give her some privacy. My brother is now in the kitchen drinking my beer. He must see something on my face because his body gets tense.

"What happened?" he asks.

Sighing, I grab the beer out of his hand and drink the rest down.

"She has scars, brother. Dozens of them on her back. Most of them are old and healed over but a handful are fresh. Hours fresh," I tell him.

Gone is my kind-faced brother and in his place is a man who could scare away the bravest of men. Don't let his friendly personality fool you. Sometimes I think Hawk is more dangerous than me.

"I know," I tell him. "I'm going to get answers. But, for now, I need to go at it alone. Rose is too fragile for a group meeting. Head home and get some sleep. Then go check the clubhouse. I want those bugs found and sent to Slim yesterday."

Hawk grabs his keys off the table and starts for the door. Halfway there he stops and turns to look at me.

"Rose? I thought she didn't have a name?" he says.

"She does now."

"Be careful, Bear. You're getting awfully close to this woman in just a matter of hours. We don't know who she is or what trouble she may bring," he tells me.

Had it been any other person, I would be pissed. Hawk and I have a strong connection. Ma always said it was because we were twins and it was bound to happen. Whatever the reason, he knows me in ways I don't even know myself.

Walking over to him I grab his left shoulder while he grabs my right and I lay my forehead against his.

"I understand what you're saying, and I'm being cautious. I just can't explain what's happening in here," I say as I point to my head. "I don't understand it myself. But I do know that this woman is meant to be here. She is meant to be under my protection. The protection of the Infernal Sons. And yes, I know what you're thinking. It is strange that she shows up at the same moment we find out we have a rat. Hopefully, I can get some answers to put our minds at ease."

"I trust you brother. We all do. I'll head over to the clubhouse now and start my search. Let me know if you need me before church tomorrow. Your bikes key is by the door." Hawk says and then walks out the door and to his truck.

Hearing Rose's soft footsteps coming down the hall I turn just as she walks into the kitchen.

Fuck, her soup.

I reach in the fridge and pull out the vegetable soup Ma brought over this morning. I empty the container into a pot and shove it on the stove to warm up. Turning back around I see Rose is standing by the table.

"Have a seat sweetheart. I'll have your soup ready in a few minutes," I tell her with a smile.

I watch her as she slowly sits at the table. Once she's seated, she places her hands in her lap and looks down. I don't like that one bit, but I hold my tongue. With her soup hot, I bowl it and place it in front of her.

"What would you like to drink, Rose?" I ask her, using her name on purpose. "We have orange juice, milk, water or beer."

"Water, please." She says quietly.

Grabbing a bottle of water, I sit it beside her bowl and take a seat across from her. Her head is still down, and her hands are still on her lap.

"You should eat," I tell her. "It will help warm you up."

Still, she doesn't move.

"Baby," I say, "please eat."

"Are you not hungry?"

"I've already had my dinner," I tell her. "Eat your food. Ma's homemade vegetable soup is amazing."

As soon as she was finished eating, I walked her to the couch to relax while I cleaned up.

"I have your room ready for you if you want to get some rest," I say as I sit down beside her. "We can talk tomorrow."

She nods.

"First, I want to put some cream on those cuts. A few look like they could be infected." She gives me a nod again, and I walk her to her room.

"Hop in bed and get under the blankets," I tell her. "Lay on your stomach and raise your shirt."

I walk to the bathroom to grab the first-aid kit I keep

under the sink. By the time I get back to her room, she is in bed on her stomach with the blanket covering her from her hips down. She has her shirt raised above her shoulders, and my anger returns in full force.

Her entire back is covered in scars. More than I first thought when I saw it in the bathroom. There isn't much untouched skin. I grab the healing and pain cream from my kit and apply it to the few new marks as gently as I can. I can feel her small jerks and her choppy breathing, but she isn't making a sound.

I'm hurting her.

"I'm so sorry baby," I tell her. "I know it hurts but this will help."

I feel the backs of my eyes sting. The thought of this woman in so much pain breaks my heart.

Finally finished with the last cut I tape gauze over each one and lower her shirt. I grab all the extra pillows and place them beside her while gently helping her roll over on her side with her back resting against the pillows.

"Try not to sleep on your back," I tell her. "My room is right beside this one. You're safe here. Get some rest, and we will figure everything else out tomorrow, okay?"

"Thank you, Bear," she says softly.

I give her a smile, lean in and kiss her forehead. "You're welcome, beautiful."

After making sure everything is locked up, I head to my room. Usually, I sleep naked, but I wear shorts to bed tonight. The second my head hits the pillow, I'm out.

That is until the most terrifying screams I've ever heard wake me.

# Chapter Five

*Rose*

I'm stuck in my past. I know I'm having a nightmare but no matter how hard I pinch myself I can't wake up. Not until the very end. I never wake until the very end. It's like fate wants me to relive my painful existence over and over again. Every night it's a different moment from my life. It's never in any kind of order, and I always know it's a dream. I know because the fear my dream self fears isn't anywhere near as frightened as I actually was. The pain my dream self feels isn't close to the real pain I felt. But, I'm still afraid and I still hurt. Tonight's nightmare is about the day before. Hours before I finally made my escape.

*I hear my father's voice outside my locked door. He isn't speaking loud enough for me to understand what he's saying but he does sound excited. After he's finished speaking, I hear a new voice. Father has brought very few people to this part of his home. He never wanted my face to be well known. He never said why, and I knew better than to ask.*

*Hearing the key slide into the lock I quickly walk over and sit on the chair by my window. Head down, hands in my lap. I don't want to make my father upset, today. I'm still healing from my previous mistake.*

*"Girl, make yourself presentable and come to my office. You have three minutes and not a second more," my father informs me. "Wear the blue dress."*

*Hearing the door shut I jump up and run to my closet. Tearing off my clothes as fast as I can as I yank the desired dress from the hanger and slide it on. After making sure everything was on correctly, I run to the small bathroom attached to my room and brush my hair.*

*A little over two minutes left. I go to my door and knock knowing Eric, my prison guard, will be waiting. Once Eric opens the door I walk as fast as I can to father's office. It's down the stairs and on the other side of the house. Reaching his office, Eric knocks.*

*"Enter," father says.*

*Eric opens the door and stands aside. I walk in and go to stand at my father's desk. As are the rules. Head down, hands folded in front of me.*

*"Eric, I need you to go and pick my son up at the airport. He's expecting you," Father tells my guard. I hear a "yes sir" before the door is closed.*

*"Ten seconds to spare," he says. "Well done, girl." I stand in the silence while I feel my father just staring at me. He's been doing that a lot lately. He's never done anything like it before and it's a bit unnerving.*

*I hear someone clear their throat from the back of my father's office.*

*"Oh, right. Girl, I want to introduce you to Roman Hernández," my father says. "Use your manners and introduce yourself."*

*I'm confused and so afraid. Father has repeatedly said my face was to be hidden until I turned twenty-five. I'm twenty-four. My birthday is tomorrow. I've always wondered why I had to stay hidden. Does this Hernández person have anything to do with it?*

*Turning around I make certain to keep my eyes cast down and my hands in front of me.*

*"Good evening, Mr. Hernández," I say. My voice is shaky and barely above a whisper.*

*"Angel. You were right, Brian. Voice and body of an angel. I wonder, do you possess the eyes of one as well?" Roman questions as he tips my face upward.*

*I'm trying to keep my eyes on the floor, but my head is tilted up too far, so I just look at Roman's shirt instead.*

*"Let me see your eyes," Roman demands.*

*Too afraid to look him directly in his eyes I settle for his nose. I can see his sinister smile. I don't like the way he's looking at me. I have a bad feeling about this man. Could he possibly be any worse than father?*

*"Yesss," he hisses. "Eyes so dark I can see my reflection."*

*He releases me and walks toward my father.*

*"The contract states that the day she turns twenty-five the deal will be set into place. I assume all of the stipulations are in order?" Roman asks my father.*

*Deal? What is he talking about? What stipulations?*

*"Of course, Mr. Hernández," Father says. "Everything is as it should be. The girl will obey, and she is pure."*

*What? Obey? Pure? Oh no. Please don't be what I think this is.*

*"Excellent, I'll be back in the morning to pick her up," Roman tells my father.*

*"NO!" I scream.*

*Both men freeze and stare at me in shock. I know I've messed up big time by speaking out, but I can't leave with that man. My life will become even worse than it already is.*

*"What did you just say, woman?" Roman asks me. His voice is too calm. My heart beats faster.*

*"I'm not going anywhere with you," I scream. At least, I did in my head, but the words came out more like a squeak.*

*"Girl, I suggest you shut up this instant. Mr. Hernández will not be as lenient as I have been," father tells me.*

*"I'm not leaving with him, father. What kind of deal did*

*you make?" I ask.*

*"None of your..."*

*"ENOUGH," Roman yells.*

*I brave myself up enough to look into his eyes and what I see has my body shaking and my skin damp. His eyes are full of anger...and lust.*

*"Perhaps I ought to teach you something myself before I leave. What say you, Brian? Should I teach my new toy a lesson?" Roman holds my gaze while speaking to my father.*

*"I think it might be a good idea. I can show you the punishment room," father tells him.*

*Roman walks forward and grabs me by the back of the neck and squeezes hard enough to leave bruises. He then shoves me along with him as we follow Father to the room I hate the most.*

*We're now standing at the back of the basement right in front of a red door marked private. Father opens the door and I'm shoved inside.*

*"You know the drill girl," father says.*

*I don't beg my way out of it. My attempt would be futile. I remove the blue dress and stand by the single table waiting for instructions.*

*"Such beautiful skin," Roman says with a low voice. "Your back is marked almost perfectly. How about I add my own signature? Go against the wall and place your hands where the chains are."*

*My eyes are stinging as I walk to the back wall, but I refuse the let the tears fall. I raise my arms and place my hands in the thick cuffs while Roman locks them in place. I spread my feet until they are placed in the correct spot. Roman slides his hand all the way down my body until he reaches my feet and locks them into place.*

*"I like your toys, Brian. But I brought my own," Roman*

*says.*

*I feel the first cut. It surprised me because there was no warning. Roman said nothing before he pushed the blade in my back. Father always yells at me while he plays. Roman just remains silent. I refuse to scream, but a whimper does escape. I feel the tip of the knife in a different spot and brace myself for more pain.*

*This time he pushes so hard that the knife went deeper than any blade ever has. No matter how much I hated to give him the satisfaction, I scream. He did this several more times. Once or twice the blade went so deep I could have sworn it touched bone. My body is exhausted, and I can no longer hold my own head up.*

*Roman walks in front of me, roughly grabs my chin and forces it up.*

*"Eyes," he demands.*

*I look up into his eyes and see joy looking back at me. With his other hand, he grabs me between my legs.*

*"You are my property, angel. You will always do what I say when I say it. Let this be a lesson. Next time I won't be so gentle." He drops my face and walks away. "Release her, Brian. Send her to her room, and I'll be back tomorrow to claim what is mine."*

*"You got it, Mr. Hernández."*

*Father releases the locks and I fall to the ground knowing I can't stay there but a few seconds. I use what strength I have left to stand and walk behind father as he leads me back to my room. I don't dare put the dress back on because I wasn't told I could. I have on my panties and nothing else as I stumble from room to room. Not a single person we pass saying a word. They never do.*

*I walk inside my room, and the door is slammed shut. I know I will get no help, so I do what I always do and head to the bathroom to take a cold shower. The cold water always helps a little with the pain and washes away most of the blood.*

*As I'm standing in the shower that's when it hit me. Eric isn't here. He went to pick up Josh. I didn't hear the lock slide into place when father shut the door. He has a key but he's usually not the one to make sure I never leave my room. Eric is.*

*My heart is racing as I turn the water off and throw on the thin nightgown I have hanging by the shower. I don't even take the time to dry off. I go to the door and send up a silent prayer. Placing my hand on the handle, I twist, and the door gives way and cracks open. I don't think, I just go. Being cautious and looking around to make sure I'm alone I dash down the stairs, ignoring my pain, and run for the back door.*

*I reach it and step outside. It's dark. Very dark and bitterly cold. But I don't care. I run. I run with everything I have toward the town I know is only a few miles away. I know I don't have long before someone notices.*

"Rose, oh god, baby please wake up."

I know that voice.

I open my eyes and realize that I'm screaming. Forcing myself to stop, I stare at Bear in shock.

"I'm so sorry," I tell him.

"You have nothing to be sorry about. You were having a nightmare," he says as he gently touches my face. "I couldn't get you to wake up."

The brief glimpse in his eyes tells me he was worried. No one has ever been worried about me before. I lose what little control I had left and cry. Bear picks me up as if I weigh nothing, sits down with his back to the headboard and lays me on top of him. He holds me tight and for the first time in my life, I feel safe. I don't know how long he held me while I cried but I eventually found the strength to stop.

"Do you want to talk about it?" he asks me.

I don't want to tell him anything about my past, but I know I need help if I want to stay away from my father and Roman Hernández. I also trust Bear. I don't know why. I've only known him for a handful of hours, but I feel it deep in my bones that he can save me.

So, I shake my head no and say, "yeah."

# Chapter Six

*Bear*

Laying on my back with Rose on top of me would typically have me thinking of ways of getting the woman under me. However, the current situation feels anything but sexual. Rose is silent for so long that I thought she fell asleep. Then her soft voice breaks the silence, and she finally opens up.

"I've never met my mother. For as long as I can remember it's just been me, my father, and his people," she says in a timid voice.

"His people?" I ask.

I feel her nod against my chest.

"Yeah, the people who work for him."

I lock away that info for another time and wait for her to say more.

"My father is very strict, and he doesn't like it when his rules are broken."

She's silent for a few minutes, and I feel her body start to shake.

"You're safe here." I hold her tighter trying to prove to her that I'll protect her. "You don't have to say anymore if you don't want to."

"It's fine. I really need help, Bear. I don't know what to do," she tells me through shuddering sobs. "Maybe I can go to the police. Aren't they supposed to help with things like this?"

"Let's go through it together first. Then I'll discuss it with my brothers, and if we need to, we'll involve those idiots, okay?"

"Um, okay. As I said, it's always been just my father and me," she tells me as her body softens against mine a little. "Well, I guess that's not entirely true. I have a younger brother. His name is Josh. He never lived in the house with us, but he was around often."

Rose lifts her head up, places her chin on her hands, and stares down at my chest. While I ache for her to look into my eyes, I can't be too upset at the moment because I can now see her face as she talks.

"Josh was nice to me every chance he could be," she says with a small smile. "He couldn't let father see, but when we were alone, he was always so kind. He would even sneak me in a chocolate bar every so often. The ones with nuts. Have you heard of them?" She asks and takes a quick glance up at my eyes. "They are so very good."

"I have," I say. I chuckle at the look on her face. I'm getting this woman all the chocolate bars she desires.

"Anyway, Josh lived with his mother. I'm not sure where, but I do know it was far."

Sighing, Rose lays her head back down on my chest.

"From the time I was little, I knew never to break father's rules for if I did, I would end up in the punishment room."

"Punishment room?"

"The name itself is pretty self-explanatory. Father isn't one for his imagination. He calls things for what they are," she says as if she's just stating a simple truth.

"What happens in the punishment room?" I ask her, trying to keep my rage checked.

"It depends really on what I did. Sometimes I just got left in there for hours, or days with no food or water. Father would always turn the heat up on those days. Other times I was tied down on this metal table, naked, and father would play with my skin using dry ice."

"What?" I yelled.

"Hours, I would be held there while he traced my skin with the ice, and sometimes, the pain would be worse than the cuts," she continues as if she didn't just hear my sudden outburst. "Occasionally, he left them in one place too long, and it burned my skin so badly it scarred. You've seen my back, Bear," she rolls off me, sits on the bed beside me, and finally looks me in the eyes.

"He would cut me with his knife and leave it to become so infected that it scarred terribly. I have marks on my side where he would shoot me with that electric gun he has, and they have scarred terribly. The marks on my back carry down to my inner thighs. Burns on my stomach and legs from the dry ice. Don't you see it, Bear? I will never be a beautiful Rose. I will never be a beautiful anything. I am scarred on the inside just as bad, if not worse, as I am on the outside. Not to mention my father sold me to some man named Roman Hernández. So, can you please just let me get out of your hair and take me to the police?"

I lay there shocked silent. The more she spoke the more confident her voice became. Sweet Rose will be one fierce woman once she blossoms. Then it hit me. Did she just say what I think she did?

Finding my voice, I ask, "Did you say, Roman Hernández?"

"Yes," she says with a resigned sigh as she slumps easily onto her side.

"Let me tell you a little more. My father's number one was rule was that I was to never show myself to any of his company. My face was not to be known to anyone but my brother, the workers, and father. I never really understood why. I also never asked. Then last night father brought a man home and told Eric to bring me to his office."

"Wait, who is Eric?" I ask before she can continue. I want to make sure I have all the facts.

"Oh, Eric was my prison guard. He was the one who was always guarding my door, walking me from room to room, watching me while I was outside."

She pauses as if in thought then continues where she left off.

"I go to fathers office, and I'm told that I will be leaving with Roman Hernández the next morning. Something came over me and I shouted that I wasn't going anywhere. Mr. Hernández decided to teach me a little lesson before he left. That's why the marks on my back are so fresh."

Just another reason to kill Hernández, slowly.

"Roman and my father were talking about a deal that was due to be set on my twenty-fifth birthday. I had to be pure and able to obey or something of that nature,"

I wait a few minutes before speaking.

"Okay, let me start off first by asking when your twenty-fifth birthday is?"

Peering at me under those long eyelashes she says, "Today. I guess that's why Roman had to leave and come back in the morning because whatever deal they had made had yet to start."

It's her birthday?

"I know Roman Hernández," I mutter.

Rose's eyes widen with fear, and I knew I made a mistake in my word placement. Again. Reaching out I tuck her hair behind her shoulder.

"No, baby. I know of him. I know who he is. He's not

a friend. Hernández is the Mexican Drug Lord for the Hernández Cartel. I can't tell you much because that's club business, but my brothers and I have been looking into him for some time now. He's bad news. I'm glad you found a way out when you did. Is there anything you can tell me about him?"

"His eyes shine with lust when he's cutting into my skin, and he seems to think I belong to him. He has a very evil smile, and I fear him more than I do my father. Apart from that, I know nothing about the man. I was only around him for a little while."

I didn't think she would be able to tell me any more than I already knew, but what she did tell me had me adding a little bit more pain to Hernández before he takes his last breath.

"Okay, here's what we're going to do. Some of the brothers will be over here in a few hours for a meeting," I tell her. "After that, we will make a trip over to the clubhouse because I have a few things I need to take care of. Then I'm taking you to Ma's."

"Your mothers? Why would you do that?" she asks.

"Multiple reasons. One, she finds out your here, and I didn't bring you there, she will pull my ear in front of you and the whole club until I lose my man card," I say, and she giggles. If me losing my man card to my Ma causes her to giggle, I will do it daily, and with a smile on my face. "Two, it's your birthday baby, and Ma makes the best cakes. So, I'm giving her a call now, so she can be ready."

"Oh, you don't have to do anything like that. It's just a silly day when I turn another year older," she says with a sad smile.

"You've never had a birthday party before, have you?" I ask her.

Looking down at the pillow she shakes her head.

"Roll to your stomach. I'm going to apply more cream. Then we eat breakfast, and I have a meeting, we head to the clubhouse, and then go to Ma's. Sound good?"

"Yeah"

"Good, be right back," I tell her.

I go to my room and grab my phone before heading to the back porch. I find the contact I want and hit dial.

"What are you doing calling me at this hour when you have a guest in your home?"

"Ma, who told you I have a guest?" I ask, already knowing what suck up twin it was.

"Hawk told me all about your pretty, scared, lady friend. He said you were acting all protector around her. I think it's sweet. What can I do?"

That's my Ma. Always wanting to help.

"Actually, I just found out that today is her birthday. She's twenty-five. She's never had a party before, Ma. She's never really had a good family. Don't do anything overwhelming. Just something to make her feel special."

"Oh, honey," Ma sniffs. "I have the perfect idea."

"I mean it, Ma. She's very skittish. It doesn't take much to scare her. We'll be over this evening. I have club business to take care of."

"She's skittish, and you're taking her to the clubhouse?" Ma asks.

"She'll be with me the whole time, and when she's not she'll be with Hawk. I have it all planned out. Be there later. Love ya, Ma."

"I love you, too, son. Don't worry. I will have everything ready. I can't wait to meet your new special friend."

Hanging up with Ma, I grab the cream and head back to Rose.

# Chapter Seven

*Rose*

I'm sitting in Bears room watching some reality show about women choosing wedding dresses. Bear told me his friends would be over soon for a meeting and I wasn't allowed to listen in, so he walked me to his room, told me to sit and watch television until they were finished.

That was about an hour ago...and I really have to pee.

The bathroom is just down the hall, but I don't want to accidentally overhear anything being said. Bear has been nice, so far. I don't want to risk not listening to him and being punished. Or worse. Thrown out.

Wiggling on the bed, I realize I don't have a choice. If I run, I can make it before I embarrass myself. I'll just hold my ears and hum a soft tune. I open the door, hold my hands over my ears and rush quickly to the restroom shutting the door behind me.

After relieving myself and washing my hands, I head back toward Bears room. Reaching my hands up to cover my ears I pause half-way when I hear an unexpected name.

"Josh Pierce called the clubhouse this morning asking about her."

Josh? Why would he be calling here? How does he even know where I am?

"What did he want?" I hear Bear ask.

"He said he just wanted to talk to her. Just to hear her voice for himself and make sure she was alright. I told him to call back later, and he could talk to you."

"Yeah, that was a good call. Her father knows who she's with. Now, knowing her story, I wish I didn't make such a rash decision last night in taunting the man," Bear grumbles. "Speaking of her father, Chains, any update on who he is?"

"Yep, I figured it out. But, didn't you just ask her?" Chains asks.

"No, I was going to this morning, but she woke up from a nightmare. It was a memory from her past. From what I've learned so far, her life has been hell. She's been nothing but her father's prisoner her whole life."

"It wouldn't have mattered," I quietly say as I step in the kitchen.

"Rose."

"I'm so sorry, Bear," I say to the floor. I can feel the tears trying to fight their way out. I'm so afraid. "I've been watching television for a very long time now and I had to use the restroom. I promise I tried my best not to hear. It was only on the way back to your room that I heard my brother's name."

"Oh sweetheart, come here," Bear says, as he reaches out his hand.

With only a moment's hesitation, I go to where he stands and he wraps me in his arms.

"I'm not mad, sweet Rose," Bear says as he gently raises my chin until my face isn't hidden by my hair.

"Whoa, who are you and what have you done with our grumpy President?" One man says.

"Shut the fuck up, Ink," Bear grunts.

Hearing the men around the kitchen laugh, I can't help but let out a small giggle. As scary as this group of men may seem they feel like a family. A family that loves each other and would do anything for each other. I've never felt this before. While I know I'm not part of their family, I close my eyes and let myself pretend I actually mean something special to this group of scary looking, soft-hearted men.

"What did you mean when you said it wouldn't have mattered?" Bear asks.

My eyes are still closed, and I feel his fingers tracing my jaw. The darkness behind my eyes always makes me feel safe when the unknown tries to break down my barriers.

"I don't know much about Father. Apart from his name, physical description, favorite form of punishment, and his rules, I couldn't tell you anything else," I say.

"Your father, Brian Pierce, is in the running for Governor of Ohio," Chains says. "I knew I'd seen his face before. He was a mess last night, but it was the hair. Same as yours. Super light blonde. Almost white. I've seen him on those posters all over town."

"Father wants to be Governor?" I ask.

"You didn't know?" another of the men asks me.

Looking down at the floor, I say, "no, like I said I don't know much about him. I do know he spends most of his time away from home and when he is home he's mostly in his office."

"Alright, we'll figure more out later. Let's head to the clubhouse and see if Slim has come up with anything," Bear says. Knowing they have been dismissed, everyone stands up and leaves.

"Oh! I'll be right back," Chains says before he runs out the front door.

"You good, baby?"

"Um, yeah, I'm okay," I whisper.

"No, you're not, but you'll get there." Bear gives me a

long hard look. "I really like you in my shirt," he tells me with a grin.

Chains rushes back into the house holding a black overnight bag before I can respond. Not that I would know what to say.

"My sister, Laura, sent over some things for you, Rose. I'm not sure what all she threw in here, but there should be some clothes. She's very tall, so I know they won't fit, but I did tell her how small you were, so she probably did her woman thing and figured it out."

"That was so very kind," I tell him. "Please, thank her for me."

"You got it," he says with a wink.

"You go on and get changed while I close the house down," Bear tells me.

I nod my head and look at the bag that Chains is still holding. Knowing I need the bag but having the courage to walk over to the man and get it are two different things. Bear must have sensed my struggle because he walks over and grabs the bag, walks back and grabs my hand and walks me back toward the bathroom.

He tosses the overnight bag on the floor just inside the bathroom and gently nudges me inside.

"Take your time, sweetheart. I'll be waiting for you," he says before he closes the door.

I open the bag and the first thing I see is a smaller bag right on top. Looking inside I see it's full of toiletries. Laying it on the sink, I look back in the bag for clothes. Not wanting Bear to wait too long, I grab the first thing I see. It's jeans and a plain light pink shirt. Digging a little deeper I see a black cardigan. Perfect.

I pull Bears shirt over my head and turn to examine my back in the mirror above the sink. It still hurts dreadfully but the bleeding has stopped, and the swelling seems to be going down. I make sure all the bandages that Bear has placed are secure before I put on Laura's clothes.

There's a knock on the door just as I'm putting my head through the top.

“There's another bag out here on the floor that Chains forgot about. I'll be in the kitchen when you're finished,” I hear Bear say before his heavy steps walk away.

I finish dressing, not forgetting the cardigan, because I'm already cold, and open the door to get the other bag. Opening it, I see that it's shoes, and I grab the black boots. They seem like the only pair that will fit me enough to not fall off my feet.

I grab the brush in the smaller bag and brush my hair. It being the first time since being summoned to my father's office since I did so, it's a mess. My hair is thick and hangs about half-way down my back, so it takes me a few minutes to work through all the tangles that have made themselves at home on my head.

I'm so thankful that Chains' sister thought of everything. I do quick work of pulling my hair up and tying it back with a black hair tie that was on the brush handle.

Walking out of the bathroom, I already feel better than I have in a long time. It's amazing what a good outfit will do for your confidence. I stop when I see Bear leaning against the wall right by the bathroom.

“Oh! Hi. I'm ready,” I say.

“My god, you're beautiful,” he mumbles back.

I can feel myself blushing.

Chuckling, Bear says, “did you know that when you blush your freckles get darker?”

I shake my head and suddenly wish I would have kept my hair down. I have nothing to hide behind now.

"Let's go, baby. The brothers already left and will be waiting for us."

We walk outside, and we head to the back of his cabin where a garage sits that I didn't see last night. He opens its door, and there sits a bike.

Oh my!

Bear walks over to me and shoves a helmet onto my head. I was so focused on the thought of having to ride on that thing I never even see him move.

Sitting on his motorcycle, he says, "hop on," and pats the seat behind him.

Shaking away the fear, I walk toward the bike.

"Maybe I should go see if Chains' sister sent over some thicker clothes," I say.

"What you have on is fine. Just climb on and scoot as close to me as you can," he tells me.

Well, okay then. I hop on the bike and scoot forward. Bears back is a solid wall of man heat. Which I'm not complaining about. He starts his bike, tells me to hold on tight and then we are off.

At first, it was terrifying going so fast. I wasn't used to vehicles with doors on all sides let alone something so small with no door to protect me if I fell sideways. I squeezed my eyes shut with my face planted in Bears back while holding him as tight as I could. Eventually, I felt relaxed enough to open my eyes.

Wow! This is amazing. In a moment of bravery, I throw my hands up in the air and laugh. While I felt dizzy from everything flying by so fast, I also felt something for the first time in my life.

I felt Free.

# Chapter Eight
## *Bear*

Hearing Rose laugh and let loose on the back of my bike is my new favorite sound. The fact that I make her feel safe enough, to feel so carefree, makes my chest puff out with pride. The ride from my cabin to the clubhouse will take us only fifteen minutes.

I live in the Deerfield Countryside of Lebanon, Ohio. It's roughly thirty minutes outside of Cincinnati. The Infernal Sons clubhouse is somewhere between my cabin and the edge of the city. I love my club and my brothers. I would die for them, but I needed a place far enough away that I could go regroup if need be and still be close enough if I needed to get there fast. If I push her, this beauty could likely get me there in five.

Rose's arms wrap back around my waist and she squeezes tight. Only then do I speed up.

Reaching the clubhouse, I slow my bike to a stop and hop off.

"Stay by my side unless I say otherwise, understand?" I tell a wide-eyed Rose.

"Is it safe in there?" she asks, still sitting on the bike.

"Yes, but some of the brothers had a party last night and are probably hungover. Hungover brothers have less mouth filter than sober brothers. They won't hurt you, baby. However, they are men and you are achingly beautiful. So, just stay by my side, yea?"

I trust my brothers with my life. I'll trust them with Rose's life. I, however, don't trust them not to try and get between her sweet legs the first chance they get. I'll be damned if I let anyone touch what's mine. There's no point in fighting it. I can feel the pull toward her, and I'm not a fucking boy who plays games. If I see something I want, I go for it.

When this tiny, pale-skinned, freckled-faced, frightened angel ran into my bar last night, both of our fates were sealed. Now, I just need to stop the bastard who's hunting her and make her fears go away.

I help her off the bike and hold on to her shoulders to keep her steady. The first few times on a bike is a shock to the body. Seeing she's steady, I give her a small smile and put my hand on her back to guide her forward.

The first thing I notice when we walk inside is that all the brothers are hanging around the couches and eating. Then I notice something that pisses me the fuck off.

"What the fuck are the bunnies doing here?" I yell.

Every head turns in my direction. Rose makes a small noise and pushes her small body closer to mine. Wrapping my arm fully around her, I hold her tight.

"I said, what the fuck are the bunnies doing here? Someone better answer my fucking question."

"There was a party last night, Prez."

Looking at the man who was stupid enough to answer my question, I say, "there was a party...last night. It is now almost three in the afternoon. Listen up, because this will be the last time I repeat myself. There are to be NO... bunnies...in the fucking clubhouse...during the fucking day. Am. I. Clear?"

"Yea, Prez."

"Get them out...Now!"

Taking a deep breath in to calm myself, I look at Rose.

"It's all right sweet Rose," I smile down at her shaking

body. “I got you. Come on, let's grab something to eat.”

We walk toward the kitchen when I'm stopped by a female body pressed against my front. She boldly grabs me over my denim pants and caresses her hand up and down my bulge.

“Hey there sexy, why don't ya take me back to your room and we can have a repeat of last time.”

“Carrie...move,” I growl.

Rose tries pulling away from me, but I'm not having that one bit. Squeezing her a little tighter I use my other hand to remove Carrie's grabby one.

“Leave.”

“I didn't know ya had a sister, Bear. She's awfully pretty. She can keep the guys entertained long enough for me to give ya what ya need. I'll do that thing with my tongue that drives ya wild. Blondie here don't mind, do ya sugar?”

Any other time I would have rushed her upstairs to my room and had her on her knees. Carrie is the only bunny I fuck these days. Only one for the past year. I told her from the start I wasn't looking for an ol' lady, I wasn't looking to settle down with her. She said she was fine with it. She even spreads those long legs for the other brothers whenever they ask. It doesn't bother me one bit.

We respect our women. Ol' lady's, the women in a long-term relationship with a patched brother. Club bunnies, the women who willingly come around during parties or downtime and give her time and body freely to any brother.

Then there's Princess. We rescued this girl from an abusive home last year. Her father was a sadistic fuck. He tried getting her pregnant saying he was receiving messages from God. She was fourteen. Luckily, we got her out, and she's been with us ever since. I keep telling her she doesn't have to work for our protection, but I've given up hope in trying to make her see sense. She keeps the brothers fed most days.

We protect our bunnies; we respect them, but they are our entertainment. Not members of my club. The only females allowed to be here during normal hours are ol' lady's, Princess, Ma, and now my sweet Rose.

"OUT...NOW!" I yell.

That got her moving. With Carrie finally running out the door, I take Rose over to meet Princess and get something to eat.

"Have a seat, baby," I tell her.

I can't help but chuckle as she tries to scoot into the chair. She's so tiny. Even fifteen-year-old Princess is taller than Rose.

"Hey there, Bear." Speaking of Princess.

"Hey, Princess," I grin.

"I told you to stop calling me that. I'm way too old to be called Princess. Can't I have a super awesome name like Claws? Or I would even be happy with Kitten," Princess grumps.

"Not gonna happen, Princess," Hawk says as he flops on the other side of Rose. "You don't get to pick your own club name. It's not how it works."

"Didn't you and Bear pick your own club names?" she asks.

I hear Hawk chuckle before he says, "Nope, they were picked before we were born. Bear and Hawk are our middle names."

"How would you feel about making a couple of extra plates, Princess?" I ask.

"I'm on it," she says as she walks over to where we're

sitting. "Hi, I'm Sally, but the boys here call me Princess."

"Hello."

Princess waits a few seconds before she speaks again. "Well, girl, is there something I can call you?" Princess says with a small giggle.

Rose goes from relaxing with a small smile to deathly pale and sitting up straight, her hands folded onto her lap and her gaze to the floor.

What the fuck?

I'm standing in front of her before I can form my next thought. Pulling her hair behind her shoulder with one hand and grasping her chin with the other, I lift until she's eye level with me.

"Talk to me," I demand.

"It's just a silly reaction. I'm fine. I promise," she whispers.

"Tell us what caused the reaction, so we make sure it doesn't happen again," I hear Princess say. There is a small age difference, but maybe Princess and Rose can help each other out. They both have pieces of shit fathers.

To my surprise, Rose reaches out and grabs my hand and squeezes tight with both of hers before placing them on her lap. I'm both shocked and happy that she made such a bold move.

"It's just that...um...well, my father always calls me girl, and when, um, would you rather I call you Sally or Princess," Rose asks while looking at the young girl.

"I grump at the guys for calling me Princess all the time," she tells Rose before leaning in as if she's about to tell a huge secret. "But I secretly love the fact that I was cared for enough that someone gave me a nickname."

"I can understand that. So, when Princess," Rose gives Princess a small grin. "When she used the term girl, I guess I just went into a sort of trance."

"Like you've been hypnotized?" Slim asks from behind Rose. He's been standing behind her for a while now, listening.

Rose squeals and turns fast to see who's behind her. The movement costs her and she gasps.

"Be careful, baby. Don't want to make those worse," I say. "That's just Slim. He's why we had to come here before heading to Ma's."

"Oh," she whispers. Slim walks around to stand beside Princess. "Uh, no. It's not like I was hypnotized, per se. According to some books I've read, when a person is hypnotized, they are intensely focused on what they're doing but at the same time not worrying about it. When I hear certain words, voices or I know something bad is about to happen and there isn't anything I can do to stop it, I pull back mentally. I'm here physically, and my body follows the motions, but inside here," she points to her head, "I hide until it's safe. If I never did that, I would have lost myself to insanity years ago."

I stand there, my hand still in both of hers, and for the first time in my life, I'm speechless and so fucking proud. I know how scared she is. She's told me she's never seen the outside world. Even something as normal as a car ride was hard for her. Yet, here she sits, in a room full of scary-ass bikers and she talks about something so deep and emotional. Every ear was on her as she spoke. Her voice getting louder and more confident with every word.

It pisses me the fuck off this woman had to take such drastic measures to assure she keeps who she is alive. She's safe now, but inside, she doesn't realize that. She doesn't fully trust that I will do everything in my power to protect her. I have friends in high places and some in low places, too. I will pull in every favor I have. No one will harm my sweet Rose.

Clearing my throat, I pull my hand out of Rose's. Then gently place in on her back.

“Listen up. This here is Rose. Just so everyone is clear. She. Is. Mine. I so much as see an eye look at her in a way that makes her uncomfortable you will answer to me.”

“And me,” Hawk says.

“And me,” Chains adds.

I hear more club officers add in their protection and a grunt from Trigger. My chest fills with pride that my brothers will have my back and help protect my woman.

“Sweetheart, I have to go talk to Slim. I'm going to leave Hawk out here with you. You'll be safe,” I tell her.

I can see a moment's hesitation in her eyes before she squashes it.

“I can spend some time with Princess. We'll just stay right here and eat. Hawk can go with you. I'll be fine. Besides, there's that scary grunting man by the door. I'm not sure he would let a fly in here without an invitation.”

Tossing my head back I laugh. How can this woman make me full out laugh at a time like this?

“Yeah, you're right. Trigger is something of a fierce brother. You sure you'll be fine? I won't be too long,” I tell her.

“She'll be fine. Go, do your thing. We're gonna eat and pow wow! It'll be nice to have a lady my age-ish around here to chat with. Those bunnies only ever want to discuss one thing, and Ma's always trying to convince me to move in with her.”

Smiling, because I noticed Princess's lack of the word *girl* and because Ma really has been trying to get her to move in. I'm sure Ma will get her way eventually, she always does.

Without a second thought, I reach down and kiss Rose's temple. She freezes, and I just smile down at her. My sweet beautiful Rose. I plan to make her feel safe. I plan to make her feel wanted. I plan to make her feel loved. Then I plan to make her mine. In all ways.

# Chapter Nine

*Bear*

Hawk assures me that all the bugs have been removed. I trust him, so I follow him and Slim into the meeting room. Once inside I make certain the door is shut before taking my seat.

"Okay, what have we got?" I ask.

"You're not gonna like it, Prez. I found a total of eleven bugs throughout the Clubhouse. Five in here, three in the lounge area and three in your room upstairs," Hawk informs me through gritted teeth. He's on edge, and I don't think I'm calm enough myself to help him down from it.

"Slim," I say.

"Alright," Slim puts a single bug on the table. "All the bugs Hawk found were dead. This is a mini home-made wireless FM transmitter. The battery power lasts a little over an hour and it can attain proximity of roughly one-hundred feet. It's very sensitive, so it would have picked up every sound in the room."

"One-hundred feet?" I ask.

"Yep, that's about from here to the front gate," Slim tells me. "So, whoever it is that's planting these bugs are still on club property when they're listening."

"Church almost always lasts over an hour," Hawk says. "The rat most likely plants the bug on days when church is pre-planned. Drops the bug off a little early and slips out none the wiser. As for the ones found in the lounge and your room, your guess is as good as mine."

"When we're not having church, this room is always open and free to use," I say. "The rooms upstairs are always unlocked. Literally, anyone who has been in this building could have done this."

Shaking his head, Hawk says, "But, it's been done multiple times. There's no reason for someone to plant multiple bugs in one room at once. Slim said that each one was super sensitive and would pick up every sound. So, I don't think it was some random person who just popped in during a party. It's someone who's here all the time."

"So, the five bugs in this room alone were planted at five different times," I say.

I stand up and pace the room. I need to get this shit figured out. Spinning around, I look at my brother.

"You said you got all of the bugs out of this building?" I ask him.

"One hundred percent," he tells me.

"Alright, I'm calling church for tomorrow morning. Tell only the officers. I want this fucking room checked before a single word is spoken tomorrow. In the meantime, Hawk, have our other buildings checked. Vehicles, too," I say as I'm walking toward the door. "Now, I'm going to get my woman and take her to Ma's. Today's her birthday and I'll be damned if I let some rat stop me from making my sweet Rose smile."

"One more thing," Hawk says before I can open the door.

Turning around, I wait for him to speak.

"I'm happy for you, brother. I know what I said last night, but I really do have a good feeling about her. She's gonna be good for you. Good for this club. Just be gentle with her. You don't want to lose her right when you know how beautiful life can be with her in it."

Again, if it was anyone but Hawk, he would have had my fist in his face. Walking over until we're boot to boot,

I look my twin in the eyes so he can read me. So, he knows how serious I am about her. He gives me a nod; one I return.

He drops his forehead to mine, and I give myself a moment to collect my strength. The brothers are used to us Allington twins having our private moments. We've always been close, and everyone knows it.

The door slams open, and the room explodes with angry voices. Even though our church room has been fitted with soundproof everything, I'm still surprised we didn't hear a single thing.

"Prez, you need to get the fuck out here. Your woman needs you, and Princess is about to kick some serious ass," Trigger yells over the noise.

Without a second thought, I run out the door and into the lounge to search for my woman.

****Rose****

*10 minutes earlier*

***The minute Bear*** walks away, I start to panic. I know it seems silly considering I've only known the guy less than twenty-four hours. I can't explain it.

I once read a story about a woman taken by this guy named Steve Brentwood. He was a Realtor agent, and he took her to one house he knew was empty and had access to. He beat her and violated her.

Some random guy was doing his morning run when he heard her screaming. He ran inside and fought off her attacker. Anyway, skipping all the details, she fell in love with him. Obsessive love. He tried letting her down easily. He was happily married and had a family, but she had a bad case of hero-worship.

I don't think that's what's happening to me. Bear isn't the only one who saved me last night. It was Bear, Hawk, Trigger, Chains, Ink and the other man whose name I have yet to learn. Trigger, Chains, Ink and the nameless man are still in this room but the farther away Bear walks, the faster my heart beats.

“So, Rose, you do realize that you've just been publicly claimed, right?” I hear someone say.

Turning away from the door that Bear just closed I look back to see Princess sitting across from me at the table.

“Um.”

“Tell me, where did you pop up from?” she asks.

“Um,” I say again.

Giggling she asks, “you're not much of a talker, are ya?”

“I've just never really had the reason to,” I tell her.

“Reason to what?” she asks, looking confused.

“Talk,” I say. “Most of my life I've been in rooms alone or with father and his workers. Talking when I'm not asked a question was redundant.”

“Your eyes look so sad. What does redundant mean?” she asks.

The way Princess holds herself you would think she was much older than fifteen. I guess I forgot someone so young might not understand.

“It means not needed or not useful. My father is a strict man. I only spoke when he wanted me to.” I didn't want to talk about my father anymore. She must have seen something because she changed the subject.

“What are your plans today?”

“I'm not sure. I heard Bear say we came here so he

could talk to Slim and then we were heading to see his mother?"

"Is that a question?" she asks.

"Maybe?" I say. "Is it alright if I use the restroom?" I liked Princess but I really need a minute to myself.

"Of course, just down that hall. Last door on your right."

"Thank you," I said.

I found the bathroom quickly. Seeing the door is slightly ajar and the lights are off I assume that it's not occupied. Easing the door open gently, I reach my arm in and search for a light switch. Finding it and switching it on I walk in and shut the door. The second the door is shut, I'm slammed up against it, hard.

"I don't know who you think you are, but listen close," says the female voice I recognize from earlier. The same female that pressed her body right up against Bears. "Bear is my man. You might be his new toy but as soon as he realizes you're nothing but a broken piece of trash, he will toss you aside and come crawling back to me. You're nothing but a filler. Do you understand me?"

I try not to whimper. She has one hand on my head pulling at my hair and the other with her long nails digging right on top of the fresh cuts on my back. Now, my nose and left cheekbone hurt.

She pulls me back by my hair and slams my face back against the door and then screams, "I SAID, DO YOU FUCKING UNDERSTAND?"

I don't move. I'm in so much pain, but I don't move. Then my head vibrates, and I realize that there's someone banging on the door from the other side.

"Rose, what's wrong?"

Princess. I think the words, but my body is too afraid

to do anything. It's too afraid to move, too afraid to speak.

"Rose, open this damn door. RIGHT NOW!" Princess ends on a yell.

"Fuck!" The woman behind me says. Carrie, I think that's her name. "Tell them you fell," she says as she releases me and splashes water from the sink onto the floor.

I fall to the floor, crawl to the corner of the bathroom and curl my arms around my knees. I just want to go home.

I mean, Bears home. I want to go back to Bears home where I've never felt safer.

The bathroom door bursts open and Trigger walks in. He notices Carrie first, standing by the overflowing sink. I can't see his face, but I notice how his body gets tense. His head turns until he sees me and stops. I've got my head laying on my knees, and I'm trying to stop myself from shaking.

"Princess," he says.

Suddenly, I feel soft hands pulling my hair back.

"Rose, what happened?" I look up to see the concerned face of Princess.

I feel myself pulling away. It's too much for me to handle right now. I'm used to pain, but I'm not used to people, and sympathy, and strange buildings. I can hear Princess talking but I can't bring myself forward enough to answer her.

"Trigger, go get Bear, now," Princess says.

I feel her hands leave my hair, then I feel her body heat leave my side. I lean to my side and curl up in a fetal position. I just want to go to sleep for a little while.

"You fucking bitch, what did you do to her?" Princess says.

"I don't know what you're talking about. I came in here to pee and she was over in the corner like she is now." Carrie isn't a very good liar.

"Oh, bullshit. I know this is your doing. If I find out that you hurt her..."

"You'll what, little girl?"

At this point, I can't tell who is saying what. My mind is locked itself away. Its only way of protecting me.

"Here, let me show you."

"Wait, you can't touch me. I'm a bunny, I'm protected by the club."

"Oh, please, you only classify yourself as a club whore for the club's protection, but you are nothing but a no-good slut with a loose ass vajayjay."

"ROSE," a deeper voice says.

I know that voice. That voice means safety, protection. That voice is home. I try pulling my mind forward, but it won't let me. It's locked up tight.

***Bear***

***I rush out*** into the lounge and look at the spot where I left Rose. She isn't there. Noticing everyone is jammed in the hallway, I head that way.

"What the fuck is going on?" I ask.

Everyone looks in my direction then moves out of the way. Smart move. The only rooms down this hall are my office, a small storage room, and a bathroom.

"I DIDN'T TOUCH HER!" I hear yelling from the bathroom.

I run the remaining distance and what I see when I enter the room has my blood boiling. Carrie is standing with her back up against the wall, with wide fearful eyes looking at a very pissed off, red-faced Princess. Behind them, in the furthest corner of the room, is my sweet Rose. She's laying on her side in a fetal position with her face tucked into her knees.

I rush over to her and slam down onto my knees.

“Baby, what's wrong?” I ask.

I get nothing.

“Please, Rose, look at me. Talk to me. Tell me what happened.” I'm not above begging this woman.

I place my hand gently on her back and rub in small circles. She whimpers and it's then I notice her back is wet. I pull my hand away and it's covered in blood.

What the fuck?

“Why is your back bleeding again?” I ask.

“Bear?” Rose whimpers

“I’m right here. Talk to me,” I tell her.

Rose struggles to sit up so I rush to help her as gently as I can. Once she's seated, she finally lifts her head back and I get a look at her face. And I see red.

Her nose is bleeding, she has a cut lip, and what looks like the start of a nasty black eye.

I turn my head and gaze right at the bitch I know is responsible. Her face pales, her eyes grow wider and she gives me the, she knows she fucked up, look.

“Oh, yeah. You fucked up big time. Trigger, you know what to do. I'll be down in a bit.”

I can hear Carrie screaming as she's being dragged out of the bathroom and out the back door. We really should invest in some soundproof walls for down there as well.

“Let's go, baby,” I say as I stand and scoop Rose gently into my arms.

“Hurts,” she whispers.

“I know, but I'm going to take care of you,” I tell her.

Turning my head, I find who I'm looking for. "Princess, is my room ready?"

"Sure is, Bear. I flipped the mattress and put clean bedding on there a few days ago. It hasn't been slept in since," she tells me.

"Thank you."

I don't want to take Rose up to the room, to the bed, that I use mainly to fuck club whores in, but I have no choice. The first chance I get, that bed is being tossed and a new one brought in. I won't have her thinking she's anything but my forever.

"Hey, brother," Hawk says. "Why don't you two go take my room. I'll use yours for a bit. It's farther back and out of the way. Might be more comfortable for her being a little more separated from everyone for a while."

I know what he's doing, he's seen my face, read my thoughts and understood. Fuck, I love my twin. Hawk didn't bring people into his room to fuck. Besides, the type of people he's interested in rarely attend our club parties.

"Yeah, thanks, brother. Have Slim order me a new bed, would you?" I ask him.

"You got it bad, brother," he tells me back.

He has no idea.

# Chapter Ten
*Rose*

Waking up in pain is nothing new. Waking up in pain, in a strange room, is. I go to shove my face into the pillow when I'm suddenly hit with a massive amount of face pain. That's when everything starts coming back. Carrie in the restroom, slamming me against the door, twice. A feisty Princess and a very angry Bear.

"Bear," I mumble.

"He's not here, darlin'. He'll be back shortly," I hear someone say from somewhere in the room. Looking toward the voice, I see it's one of Bears friends. The one whose name I've yet to learn.

"What's your name?" I ask. Where did this bout of courage come from? I'm only ever courageous in my mind.

Chuckling, he says, "I'm Brick. Prez had to go take care of something, but he'll be back in a bit."

Brick. I now had a name to go with all six of my rescuers. Chains, Brick, Ink, Trigger, Hawk, and Bear.

I toss the blanket aside and go to stand up but fall right back down. Dang, Carrie must have used a lot of force shoving my head against that door. I am so dizzy.

"Whoa, easy there darlin'," Brick says as he walks toward me. "Where are you going in such a hurry?"

I try standing again, this time much slower. Once I'm steady on my feet I give Brick a wide smile.

"I'm going to find Bear. Where is he?" I ask.

"He's in the basement taking care of club stuff," he tells

me. "You should just wait here. He'll be back at any moment."

I have a feeling I know what *club stuff* he's up to, and I can't let him do something like that because of me.

"The basement you say," I smile sweetly up at Brick. "So, that means not one, but two sets of stairs?"

"Yep."

Great, I'm going to tumble to my death. I really do need to rest. When father was at his worst, my days would end much like this. All I need is a little food, a hot shower and a ton of sleep. I'll be better by morning.

"Let's go, big guy, I'm probably going to need your help when I fall on my face and break it further," I tell him.

"Where are we going?" He asks cautiously. "You really should be resting."

"To the basement, of course," I look back at him as I open the door.

"The base... Now, wait a minute. You are not allowed down there," he shouts as he starts following me.

"Come on, big guy. I'm going with or without you. I'd much rather it be with you considering the chances are high I will do a full-face plant on these stairs," I say.

I'm shocked that I'm speaking to him how I am. I've never felt relaxed enough to let my inner self out. Inner me, she's brave. She's who I've always wanted to be, but she's never really been able to show herself, fully. Sometimes it feels like I have two personalities in my head.

When things get to be too much, I borrow strength from my inner self. Sometimes it's just so I won't do or say anything stupid around Father. Other times it's because I need to *check out* as I did moments ago. Mostly, I reach for her when I need a little extra courage.

But, as much as I've tried, I could never fully encompass that part of myself for fear that Father would look at my strength as defiance. Then he would have destroyed that part of me.

Inner me looks like she's refusing to go back inside now that she's free. Fine with me.

I feel this aching need to get to Bear, not only to stop him from doing something stupid but because I want to be near him. So, maybe that feeling mixed with brick's being my guard to actually guard me and not keep me in prison, like my father's guard Eric, has me relaxed.

You wouldn't think after having my face slammed against a door a couple of times would have me in a good mood, but like I've said before, pain is nothing new. Pain I can handle.

Bear killing Carrie in my name, especially for something as stupid as jealousy, I cannot.

"Brick, how long was I out?" I ask him.

"About ten minutes, darlin'. Bear left once he knew you were okay," he grumbled.

We make it down to the first floor when I see Princess.

"Oh my gosh, Rose, what are you doing out of bed?" She asks.

"Basement," is all I say.

I'm on a mission. I need to get to that basement and stop what's happening.

"Brick, which way?" I ask.

Sighing he says, "Bear's gonna kick my ass. This way, darlin'. I'm telling him you forced me."

"You do that, big guy," I tell him through my giggle. "You tell him I dragged you kicking and screaming if you have to. Just lead the way."

I follow Brick as he walks toward the back of the room and out the back door. We walk along the back of the building until we get to the edge and Brick stops. Not noticing soon enough, I run right into his back.

"Sorry," I whisper.

"Basement is down there," he tells me.

Looking around his body, I see we have stopped in front of a door.

"A... are you sure Bear's down there?" I ask.

"What's wrong, little rabbit? Are you afraid of the basement?"

"It's not exactly my favorite room in a building." I shudder thinking about Father's punishment room. It's located in the back of his basement.

Pulling up my big girl panties, I walk around Brick and open the door.

The moment my foot hits the first step, I hear a low mumble of deep voices and the higher pleas of a woman.

I rush as fast as my wobbly legs will allow down the stairs. When I get to the bottom, I freeze at what I see. Bear, Hawk, Trigger and a few unknown faces were all standing around a chained up, half-naked Carrie.

"Bear," I whimper quietly.

He must have heard me because he turns fast and locks eyes on me.

"What are you doing out of bed?" He asks before turning and glaring at Brick. "And why the fuck did you bring her down here, Brick?"

"I know we've only just met your woman here, but let me tell you, she's got that innocent smile and puppy dog eyes down pat. Not to mention she didn't give a flying fuck what I had to say. She demanded what she wanted and instead of waiting she just took it."

A ghost of a smile tugs at the corner of Bear's lips.

Turning back to me, his face softens, and he asks, "Why

are you down here?"

"Before we get into that, I thought you said this was a basement," I said to Brick.

"It is," I hear from a few different people.

"No, this room is very small, cold and completely underground. It's more like cellar than a basement."

I get blank faces staring back at me.

"Okay, since we got that out of the way. Bear, you have to stop whatever it is you're doing to this woman."

That unfroze the blank faces and Bears turned into pure rage.

"I don't think so," he growls. Yes, growls. "She signed her own death warrant when she touched what's mine."

I can tell from the look in his eyes that nothing I say will change his mind. Sighing, I look up at Carrie. Her hands are tied above her head and she's dripping wet. I've been in her situation often. I know how she's feeling.

Walking up to her, I lean in to whisper.

"I forgive you."

"I don't need your forgiveness, bitch," she yells back at me.

I walk back toward Bear when I pause and look at her over my shoulder.

"You have it anyway."

I give Bear the most intense glare I can as I pass him and head up the stairs.

"My sweet Rose," follows me outside as Brick closes the door.

# Chapter Eleven

*Bear*

"My sweet Rose," I say, seconds before they close the door. Carrie attacked Rose, made her bleed and marked her body. Yet, Rose forgave her. My woman has a heart of gold. I, on the other hand, do not.

"You can't hang me in this basement like a wild animal," Carrie shouts.

"It's a cellar actually," Trigger calmly tells her.

I grin, knowing that Rose has dug herself into each brothers' hearts without even trying. It doesn't take much to care for the woman.

I look at the bitch hanging from my *cellar* ceiling. I know Rose wants me to let her go. Based on the glare she threw my way; she'll be pissed if I kill her. My grin turns into an ear to ear smile. Rose glaring at me while looking straight into my eyes turned me the fuck on. There's a fighter in her just begging to be let loose.

Just this once I'll let Rose win. Just this once.

Walking up to Carrie, I grab the chain attached to the ceiling and yank until she's face to face with me. Hearing Carrie whimper in pain makes me a happy man. Fucking bitch deserves a hell of a lot worse than she's getting.

"You're a very lucky woman, you know that?" I tell a wide-eyed Carrie. "You see, you made a mistake when you targeted Rose. Now, my plan was to make you suffer for days before I killed you." Carrie's face loses all color. "Unfortunately, you have a savior. So, here's what's going to happen. I'm going to release you and you are to leave my county and never show your face here again."

"You probably shouldn't show your face in the next three counties either," Hawk adds. "I'll be giving the clubs there a call."

"You can't do this," Carrie cries.

"Would you rather be dead?" Trigger asks with a flat tone. "I mean, I don't mind doing it for you if that's what you really want."

"No! No, please. Okay, I'll take the deal."

I unlatch the chain and release it, letting her fall to the floor.

"Get the fuck out," I tell her impatiently. This is taking way too long. I need to take care of Rose before we head to Ma's.

"I need to get my things from inside."

Hawk stares at her as if she's lost her mind. "You shouldn't have *things* here. Anything you have inside is now club property,"

"Wait," Trigger says. "How did you get back inside? I was watching the door the whole time."

I wait silently for her to answer.

"Um, I always make sure the laundry room window is unlocked. I walked around to the side of the building and crawled through the window," she says with a trembled voice.

"Go," I say, as I toss her clothes beside her on the floor.

Carrie grabs the clothes, rushes to stand and leaves quickly without dressing.

Nobody says a word until we know for sure she's far away.

"Are you thinking what I'm thinking, brother?" Hawk asks me.

"Most likely. Carrie's the one planting those bugs."

"If she is," Trigger adds. "Who was she planting them for? Because we all know Carrie isn't all that bright."

Slim steps forward from the wall he was leaning on and clears his throat.

"She's obsessed with the Prez. She could have planted them as a means to gather information to try and weasel her way into ol' lady status," Slim says. "Also, why'd you let her go if you suspect she's been spying?"

"To track her," I tell them. "She's scared. She'll contact whoever she's been spying for and ask for safety.

"What makes you think that?" asks Slim.

"Would you spy on someone like the Infernal Sons for just anyone? No, it's either for someone she knows, wants something from or fears even worse than us. Follow her, do your computer genius thing and listen in on her phone calls. I want to know every move she makes."

"Sure thing, Prez."

"Alright, I'm gonna head back up to my woman. Today's her birthday. We're heading to Ma's for a surprise party as soon as we leave. It's at six. So, get your asses together and head that way. And, someone check that damn laundry room window." I add before turning and running up the stairs.

Once inside, I head toward the kitchen, where I know Princess will be.

"Princess, today is Rose's birthday and I have Ma getting a surprise party together as we speak."

"Oh, it's her birthday? What a shitty thing to happen on your birthday."

"Yeah," I say. "She's had many shitty birthdays. Let's give her a great one this year, yeah?"

"I'll head there now and see if Ma needs any help."

"Good girl," I tell her. "Oh, and Princess, don't say shitty. It's not very ladylike."

"Fuck you, Bear," she says while trying to hold back a laugh.

I rush upstairs in pursuit of my future ol' lady.

Brick is standing outside the closed bedroom door.

"She wanted to lay down for a bit," he tells me. "She seemed a bit raddled after we left the basem... cellar," he corrects himself with a small grin.

"I say she was. Her father used to tie her up that way and it probably brought back some unwanted memories."

Bricks face loses all emotion and he clenches his fists.

"I know brother," I tell him. "We have her now. She'll never be treated like that again. Listen, head downstairs and ask Princess about today's plan. See you in a bit. And thanks for keeping an eye on her."

"No problem, Prez. You're gonna have your hands full once that woman comes outta her shell."

Smiling I say, "I know. I can't wait."

"You are one crazy son of a bitch."

"Hey," I say as I smack the back of his head. "Show some damn respect."

"My bad. You are one crazy son of a bitch, Prez," he says with a grin.

"Better."

I walk into the room and straight for Rose. I lay behind her in bed as close as I can without touching her back and lay my hand on her hip. She's too skinny. I can already hear Ma getting on my case about plumping her up.

"Are you okay?"

"What happened down there?" She asks instead of answering me.

My first thought is to say that it’s club businesses. We don't involve our women in club shit for a reason. It's too risky. Not only for the business for them as well.

I open my mouth to say just that. “I let her go,” comes out instead. What the fuck? This woman has me by the balls, and she doesn't even realize it. My jeans are getting tight just thinking about any part of her near my balls.

Rose rolls over to face me. My god, she's beautiful. Even with the black eye, and split lip.

Fuck, I should have killed Carrie.

“You let her go?” she asks. “For real?”

“Yeah, baby. I let her go. But right before she left, she said something that had me worried, so I have someone tailing her.”

“Tailing her? I'm not sure I understand.”

“It means, I have a brother following her everywhere she goes and seeing who she talks to,” I explain.

Her eyes go wide, and she gives a small nod letting me know she understood.

“What made you worry?” she asks. I want to tell her. I want to confide in this woman about everything. But this time I hold my tongue.

I hope she understands why I can't tell her. “That's club business, Baby. There are some things I won't be able to tell you. No matter how much I want to. My life isn't always safe, and the less you know about certain things the safer you'll be.”

Rose drops her eyes from mine and fidgets with the blanket. “My life is never safe, Bear. I think I will be able to handle what worries you so.”

The reminder of her past has me fuming. I hate that my sweet Rose has had such a horrible life. No, not life. She's never had the chance to live. She's had a horrible existence where she constantly fought to survive.

"I don't doubt for a second you're strong enough to handle anything thrown at you. But in this case, it's best if you don't know. At least at the moment. Please, trust me on this."

A small smile forms on those perfect lips. "I trust you on everything, Bear." Her face reddens at her admission.

I push my chest out like I'm a damn gorilla. Hearing that Rose trusts me to that extent makes me feel like a king. Fucking King Kong.

I lean forward and kiss her forehead. "Come on baby, let's get you cleaned up. We don't want to be late. Ma will have no problem trying to ground me if I'm even a minute late."

Rose let's out a small giggle as she climbs off the bed. There it is again. My favorite sound. I grab her hand once she's standing and we head downstairs.

I take Rose to the kitchen and lift her up to sit in the same chairs we were at before.

"Someone grab me the Med Kit," I yell out before looking down at Rose. "I've gotta go talk to Hawk about something. I won't be but a minute."

Her eyes grow wide with fear, and her face pales. "Can't he come over here? I will hold my ears and hum a song. I won't listen to a word that is said." Her voice is trembling. She's terrified. My brave girl from upstairs has vanished.

"What I need to ask him isn't for your ears, baby. I'll be just over there. Right by the front door. You'll be able to see me the whole time. I promise." The need to wrap Rose in my arms is overwhelming. So, that's exactly what I do. Reaching my arms out slowly, so she knows what's about to happen, I wrap my arms around her upper back where

I know there are no fresh wounds.

It takes about a minute for Rose to get her head in the game. Her stiff body relaxes, and she places her hands around my back.

"Oh my," she whispers, and I chuckle.

"Here ya go, Prez," Brick says from behind me. "It was still in Trigger's room. Don't tell him I was in there. I like being alive."

"He'll find out anyway," I say as I release Rose and reach for the kit. "The crazy fuck will notice something out of place."

"Or smell your fear," Hawk says from by the door.

"Nah, I didn't touch nothin' else. It was sittin' on the dresser right by the door," he says smugly.

"WHO THE FUCK WAS IN MY ROOM?" we hear Trigger yell from upstairs.

"Shit, I gotta go. Talk at ya later, Prez."

"Will Trigger really harm Brick?" Rose asks.

Grabbing the alcohol pads and healing cream, I turn to Rose with a smirk. "Not too bad. Brick will survive to annoy me another day." That earned me another giggle.

I finish with her bruised face and go to start on her back. Shit, I should have done this upstairs. I want no one else seeing any part of her unclothed body except me.

I slowly raise her shirt until the soiled bandages are visible. While I hate how she got them, I don't care that she's covered in scars. They just remind me of how strong my woman is.

I clean up the blood on the reopened wounds and apply cream and a new bandage before pulling her shirt back down. Leaning down, I kiss her head. "My brave girl."

"I'm going to go talk to Hawk now, I'll be just over

there."

I get a small smile. "I'll be fine, Bear."

With one last look, I turn and walk away. I need to talk to my brother. I know just what I want to get my sweet, beautiful, brave Rose for her birthday.

# Chapter Twelve
*Rose*

The moment Bear walks away, I start to hyperventilate. So much for inner me sticking around for a while. My inner courage is a coward. I'm so focused on arguing with myself that I don't notice when someone sits beside me.

"Hey there, sexy."

I spin around to see who it is and instantly lean back when I feel the stranger's breath on my face. I would have fallen to the floor if it wasn't for the man's hands grabbing onto my hips. He gives me a full tooth smile and my heart races. Not in a good way. His smile looks lustful, and everything in me is screaming to run away and hide.

"What's your name, Freckles?" he asks.

Why does everyone keep asking me that? Except this time is different because I have a name. I have yet to say it out loud, but I do have one now. Thanks to Bear.

"Um, Rose," I somehow say. Pushing the air through to answer his question was difficult. It feels as if he has his hands wrapped around my throat instead of my hips.

"Rose," he breathes. "Mmm, that tasted delicious. Do you taste as delicious as your name, Rose? I bet you do. The names Derrick. Now that we officially know one another, what do you say to taking a ride on the back of my bike?"

"Get your mother fucking hands off her before I tear them from your body," Bear says in a scary voice as he walks up behind Derrick.

Even though Bear's eyes are black with fury, I instantly

feel myself calming.

"Oh, hey, Prez," Derrick says, while still holding my hips. I try to back away, but his hands squeeze tighter.

"You have about one second to let go, or shits gonna get ugly," Hawk says. "That's Bear's ol' lady you're holding."

I glare at Hawk. Did he just call me old?

Derrick releases me as I'm figuring out how to get the courage to kick Hawk in the shin. I'll show him, old lady. Before I can react, Bear rushes forward and wraps me in his arms.

"This is your only warning," Bear growls. "Don't touch what's mine."

"Got it, Prez," Derrick says.

"What the fuck are you even doing here? You know the rules. Hang-arounds are not allowed to be here during working hours."

"I have a package for you," Derrick says. "It was delivered last night after you left. I went to my car to grab my phone when this boy runs up and hands it to me. He told me to give it to the clubs' president. I just tossed it in my car, since I knew you weren't here and decided to bring it by today."

Derrick hands Bear a small box and turns to leave.

"Well, whatever it is will have to wait. We need to get to Ma's," Bear says as he moves me to his side. "Let's go put this in my office and we'll leave." He guides me to the same hall with the bathroom Carrie attacked me in. But we stop at the first door.

I look around once we're inside. The room itself is a little bare. The only thing in here is a big brown desk with a single computer on top. The wall has a single frame. It looks to be a shadow box with a large leather vest inside.

The vest has a few random patches down one side. On the other is a small patch that says, Big Bass. Under the name is the same logo I've seen all the guys wearing. And painted on a few places inside this building.

"That was my fathers," Bear says, after seeing what I'm looking at. "He founded this club when I was seven years old. Raised me and Hawk to take over for him even though he knew it didn't work that way."

"How does it work?" I ask.

Bear walks over to me and wraps his arms around my back. I lean my head against his chest enjoying the feeling of safety.

"You don't inherit the spot of club President," he explains. "It has to be earned and then voted on by the brothers."

"I see. Then why would he train you both to take his place if it wasn't a guaranteed thing?"

"I guess Pops had hope that one day one of us would earn it," he says with a sad voice.

"Had?"

"Yeah, baby. Had. He was killed five years ago. An enemy of the club caught Pops off guard one day, and he vanished. We couldn't find a single trace of him for three months. When we finally did there was nothing the doctors could do to help. He eventually died from internal bleeding."

I wrap my arms around Bear and squeeze. "I'm sorry."

"Me too, sweetheart," he whispers. "Me too."

"Brother, I'm heading out. See you at Ma's in a bit," Hawk says from the doorway.

"Yeah, we're leaving too. Come on, time to meet my mother," Bear says

# Chapter Thirteen

*Bear*

I pull into Ma's parking lot and power off my Harley. I take a few seconds to collect myself before climbing off and turning to Rose. I've never wanted to hit a woman before but seeing the marks on Rose's face has me wanting to track down Carrie.

"You ready, baby?" I help her down.

"Yea." She reaches for my hand and swings her leg over to stand in front of me. "I'm really nervous. I don't really know what to say to people. She's going to think I'm weird."

"You talk to me just fine, and she will love you, Rose." I can already feel Ma's curious stare from inside.

"I feel safe with you, Bear," she says, softly. "I don't feel the need to hide in my shell when I'm around you. It's a scary feeling."

Well, fuck. My chest puffed out further with every word she said. "You should never be afraid of your feelings, Rose. You should always trust them. If you fear them, you might miss something important."

"Important like what?" She looks me right in the eyes waiting for my answer. I lean in and kiss her forehead. This time she doesn't tense up and that makes me so fucking happy.

"Landon Allington, who is that beautiful woman you're hiding from me?" Leave it to Ma to throw out my government name.

Placing my hand on Rose's back, because I can't seem to stop touching her, we walk toward the porch where my mother is, not so patiently, waiting.

"Ma, this is Rose." Ma has a frown on her face as she stares at Rose. I look over and see that my sweet Rose is back to looking at her feet. I reach to gently place my hand on her chin and slowly move her head up. "Rose, this is my Ma, Patty Allington."

"Hello, ma'am," Rose says with a sweet smile.

"Happy Birthday, Rose. And don't call me ma'am, child," Ma says with a stern voice, but a soft face filled with amusement. Thankfully, Rose is still looking up and can see Ma's not being mean. "Call me Ma. Everyone does."

"Oh, um...ok...Ma. Thank you." I smile at Ma knowing she will do everything in her power to make Rose feel welcome.

"Well, come on in. Gonna catch a cold out here." Ma freezes and turns a glare in my direction. "Landon, don't tell me you brought her over here on that bike of yours."

"It really was a wonderful ride," Rose says breathlessly.

Jealousy shoots through my body like a tidal wave. The only place and reason she should sound breathless is under me after I make her scream my name. Multiple times.

Fuck, I'm jealous of my damn bike.

"Why are you glaring at your motorbike, son?" Ma asks with a knowing smirk.

I turn my glare to Ma before bending over and kissing her cheek. "How ya doing, Ma?"

"I'm good, baby boy. Now get that woman of yours in the house before she freezes."

We follow Ma into the kitchen and sit at the table as she commanded.

"Rose, do you like chocolate?" Ma asks while putting

her apron on.

"Oh, yes ma'am...Ma. I love it...chocolate. It's my favorite kind...um, flavor." Rose's cheeks turn red as she stumbles through her words.

"That's good, honey." Ma's trying to hold her laugh in. Her lips are pinched but her body is shaking. "I made you a wonderful triple chocolate birthday cake."

Rose's eyes go wide, and her mouth drops open. I wait a few seconds for her to get control of her face, but it doesn't happen. With a chuckle, I reach over and push her jaw closed.

"Better be careful or a fly will make itself at home in that beautiful mouth of yours." Rose throws me a look of disgust.

"Ew."

"WHERE'S THE BIRTHDAY GIRL?" is yelled from the front door. A few seconds later Ink, Chains and Brick walk into the kitchen.

"Hey Ma, something smells fucking good in here," Chains says as he walks up and kisses Ma on the head.

"Language." Ma smacks Chains in the back with her kitchen towel. "There's a lady present."

Ink and Brick give Ma the same greeting before sitting in empty chairs at the table.

"Sorry, Ma. I'll try better." I roll my eyes knowing damn well that Chains will do no such thing.

"Everything's ready." The kitchen door that leads to the backyard opens and Princess steps inside. "Oh, hello everyone. Happy Birthday, Rose."

"Hi, Princess," Rose says with a wide smile. It makes me so happy that Rose and Princess are getting on as well as they are.

"Don't worry, the king has arrived, and the party can

begin," shouts Hawk as he and Trigger walk into the kitchen.

Ma's kitchen is by no means small, but with all of us big ass men taking up room, it's getting a little crowded.

"Logan, take this cake to the building," Ma says, ignoring his crazy twins' outburst. "Boys, head on out. Everything is all set up."

"What's going on, Bear?" Rose asks with wide eyes.

"It's your birthday, baby. We're having a party to celebrate your life." Her eyes fill with tears, but for the first time since she ran into my life, they are not tears of sadness, fear or loneliness. Those are tears of pure joy.

Before I can say anything else Princess taps Rose on the shoulder. "Happy Birthday." She hands Rose a pink gift bag decorated with white circles. "Normally gifts come later during the party, but I bought this special for now. So, Bear, go on outside, and we will meet you in a few."

I wait to make sure Rose is okay with this new development. She nods her head and I knew at that moment that everything would be just fine. My sweet Rose is a hell of a lot stronger than she thinks she is.

Entering the building, we use for get-togethers such as this, I'm not at all surprised. I told Ma not to go all out but she never listens. The room is filled with balloons, streamers, banners, and a giant sign that says, 'Happy Birthday Rose'.

"How the hell did you pull this off in such a short time?" I ask Ma who is just standing there staring at me.

"I had most of this stuff in storage. You said not to go too big. You also said she's never had a party before. So, I figured big decorations, cake and food, and a small crowd."

"You did good Ma." Wrapping Ma in my arms I let my

appreciation show.

"You gonna tell me what's wrong with that beautiful girl, Landon?" Ma steps away to look up at my face. "Why does she have fresh bruises on her face?"

"The bruises are from Carrie, Ma," Hawk says. "She got jealous and cornered Rose in the bathroom."

"I told you a thousand times to get rid of that hussy." Ma was pissed. She never did like Carrie and wasn't shy to let everyone know. Including Carrie herself. "Logan, please tell me your idiot brother is finally taking my advice?"

"She's gone, won't be coming back," I answer for Hawk.

"Good." Is all Ma says before she turns and walks toward the food table.

About ten minutes later I'm about to lose my shit and send a search party out for Rose when the door opens. Princess walks in first followed by Rose. The room is instantly quiet as everyone stops what they're doing to look at what's mine.

I allow it this time.

Rose is wearing tight jeans, knee-high black boots, and a black club sweater that Princess designed. She calls it an off the shoulder sweater. It has our club logo on the front, the front view of a motorcycle engulfed in flames. Below the logo, it says, 'Infernal Sons, MC'. Circling the logo is the quote, 'Four wheels move the body, two wheels move the soul.'

Rose has her hair in a high ponytail and the bruises on her face are gone. You can see the small cut to her bottom lip, but it was already going down.

"I figured since she was going to be a biker babe anyway, she might as well start looking the part," Princess says to the quiet room. "I wanted her to feel comfortable and to fit in. Only if she wanted to, of course. I totally asked her first."

I take a step forward, then another and another until I'm right in front of Rose.

"Hey."

"Hi," she says shyly.

"You look beautiful, Rose. You looked beautiful before, too. You could wear a trash bag and still look beautiful."

"Alright, stop making the poor woman's face burn and let's eat," Hawk says. "I'm starving."

The rest of the evening went great. It took a little while for Rose to relax but once she did it was a beautiful sight to see. She was dancing around with Princess and Ma. She was smiling, laughing. She was happy. She cried for each gift she received. I have yet to give her mine, I'm waiting a little while longer.

"She sure is beautiful, brother." Hawk stands next to me and we watch the women dance. "You're one lucky bastard."

"Yeah, sure am. We have today. She gets to be carefree and relaxed today," I tell Hawk. "Then tomorrow we need to get eyes on Roman Hernández. He's after my woman and I'm not at all happy about it."

"Agreed. Also, Brian Pierce. Rose's father won't sit idly by either. You saw the look in his eyes. He will do anything to get her back." Hawk breaks out his evil smile. "Don't worry brother, no one will take our Rose from us."

Leaning over, I punch Hawk in the shoulder. "She isn't our anything, fucker. She. Is. Mine."

"You don't have to worry about me stealing your woman, Bear. Not my type," Hawk says as he walks away.

Turning back to my woman I find that she's the only

one left dancing. Ma must have gone inside, and Princess was wrapping uneaten food.

Rose had her eyes closed and was swaying to the music with a smile on her face. I walk over to her and put my hands on her hips. She opens her eyes but doesn't stop smiling. Reaching into my pocket I pull out the gift I had Hawk pick up for me.

"Happy Birthday, baby."

"Oh, Bear. I love it," she says with fresh tears running down her face.

Laughing, I reach up and wipe her tears away. "You haven't even opened it yet. You have no idea what it is. So, how do you know you're going to love it?"

"It doesn't matter what it is. Everything...today has been the best birthday, no, the best day of my life."

Knowing that today was the best day of her life makes me both happy and pissed. How could anyone hurt this beautiful woman?

"Open your gift."

I hold my breath as she opens the box. I had to take Ma's bracelet into the shop a few months back to fix the clasp. Pops got her the bracelet before Hawk and I was born and it's her favorite piece of jewelry. While I was there, I saw this necklace with a small golden rose hanging from it. The stem and leaves were gold, but the rose petals were red gold. I haven't thought of it twice until this morning.

Rose lifts the lid and inhales. "Oh, my goodness. Bear, it's too much. I can't accept this."

"You can, and you will, sweet Rose." I grab the box and remove the necklace. Walking behind Rose, I move her ponytail to the side, wrap the necklace around from the front and clasp it in the back. Leaning down I kiss her one bare shoulder before walking back in front of her.

Rose has tears running down her face, but her eyes are alight with happiness. Looking down at her mouth, I see that beautiful smile. I can't help myself. I lean in and kiss her smiling lips. Her lips are soft and warm against mine. I leave the kiss short and sweet, not wanting to scare her. Leaning back, I look into her eyes to make sure she was doing okay. So much happiness and something a little deeper is looking right back at me.

I lean back in until our lips touch and our breaths are one. “You are mine, sweet Rose,” I breathed into her mouth. “Say it.”

“I am yours,” she whispers against my lips.

Our first kiss was one of pure joy. I will do everything in my power to make sure every kiss from here on out is the same. I can't wait to spend the rest of my days with Rose by my side.

Little did I know how soon she would be taken from me.

# Chapter Fourteen

*Rose*

A week has passed since I turned twenty-five. After we left Bear's mothers home we came back to his cabin. I haven't left since. Not that I'm complaining. It's beautiful and peaceful here. Bear goes to the clubhouse for hours a day to do what he calls 'club business', but he always has someone stay here with me while he's gone. I have yet expressed the desire to return there.

He has yet to ask.

He also hasn't kissed me since that first time. My first kiss. It was as perfect as I always dared imagine.

The past couple of days something has changed. Bear comes home, showers, tucks me into bed and goes to sleep in his room. He's quiet, and when he does speak to me it's just a couple words. Yet, every morning I wake up wrapped in his arms practically shoved under his body. I still have nightmares, but they aren't as frequent.

I'm now sitting in the kitchen drinking a glass of milk and watching the storm out the window. I'm wearing a beautiful light pink sleep gown that Bear bought me. As another birthday gift, he had bags full of clothes waiting for me when we came back to his cabin. I've never felt so cared for.

"How long have you been up?" I jump when I hear his voice. Turning, I see him leaning on the fridge wearing nothing but sleep pants.

"About an hour," I turn and look back out the window. The wind is blowing hard enough to cause the trees to sway drastically. "The storm is very angry tonight."

"Give me your eyes, baby." I take a second longer to admire the strength of the storm before turning and giving him what he's asked. It's much easier to look him in the eyes than it was when I first came here. It's only been a week, but it feels more like home than father's house ever was.

"I need to tell you something." Bear kneels in front of me, wraps one hand around the back of my neck, and places the other on my hip. I can tell whatever he has to say is serious.

"Two days ago, there was a break-in at your house. The place was trashed. Looked like whoever it was, was searching for something." I can tell there's something else, but Bear remains silent.

"What aren't you telling me, Bear?"

He scoots closer until the only thing I see is his eyes. He's holding my gaze and refusing to let go.

"Your father was killed, baby. Whoever it was that was in your home shot him while he slept."

Killed? My father is dead? In my house?

"Not my home."

"What?"

"Father's house is not my home."

Bear searches my face as if he's looking for an answer only I can give him.

"Rose, did you hear what I said?" he asks.

"Yes, you said father was dead. That he was killed."

Bear leans back and all I can do is focus on his eyes. His beautiful, warm, blue eyes.

"Sweetheart, tell me what's happening in here," he says tapping my temple.

"I think I'm a bad person, Bear."

Bear lifts me out of the chair, sits and places me sideways on his lap.

"You are as far from bad as a person can get. What's in that mind of yours that's making you come up with such a crazy thought?"

I'm afraid to say out loud how I'm really feeling, but I know Bear won't stop until I do.

"I don't feel anything." I stare down at my hands too afraid to see the disgust on his face. "You tell me my father is dead, and I feel nothing. I'm not relieved, I'm not angry or sad. I just feel...nothing."

Bear wraps his arms around me and holds me tight against his body. His arms are the safest place I've ever been. But, even now, I feel nothing.

"That's a perfectly normal reaction for someone who went through what you did at his hands," Bear says against my temple.

My only thought is how his long beard tickles my shoulder when he talks. It feels like every part of who I am went silent, and I can only focus on my shoulder. I reach up and comb my fingers through his beard.

"It's strangely soft," I whisper. "I thought it would feel rough."

"Oh, my sweet Rose. You're in shock. We're going to bed, and we'll discuss this more tomorrow if you're up to it."

"Is this why you've been acting differently for the past couple of days? I know I don't really know you, but I can tell something has been bothering you." Bear looks confused for a few seconds before his eyes grow warm with understanding.

He presses his forehead against mine. "You have no idea how much you mean to me," he whispers. He's holding my gaze and squeezing my hips tighter against his body. “If you could read my thoughts you would run in the opposite direction. I’m crazy about you, baby. I knew from the moment I met you that you were it for me.”

“Really?” I ask. To say I’m shocked is an understatement.

“Really. I’m yours, Rose. I would have had a ring on that finger the night we met if I didn’t fear it would run you off. And, as soon as you’re ready, I’m putting my baby in your belly.”

What? A baby? A ring? “Don’t you think it’s too soon for that type of conversation?” I ask him.

“Like I said, opposite direction.”

It didn’t get by me that he avoided my question. “Why have you been acting so different?”

He takes a deep breath and lets it out while pulling back to look at my face. “I’m sorry, baby. I’m trying to make you safe. There are some things you don’t know, and I’d like to keep it that way unless I think you need to know for safety reasons.”

“Things involving my father?” Just the mention of my father has my eyes lowering to my lap. “If that’s the case, Bear, he’s dead. You can tell me.”

Bear gently grabs my chin and forces my head up. “You mentioned that your father had business with Roman Hernández?”

I let out a single humorless laugh. “If by business you mean selling me to him, then yes. Why?”

“I told you before that the club has been looking into Hernández,” I nod my head not sure I’m liking where this is going. “The FBI has been trying to build a case against him for years. He’s smart. Never gets his hands dirty. Leave’s the illegal work to his lackey’s. But the thing is, baby, he made two fatal errors."

I look up into Bears eyes and notice they're very dark. Not just in color, but in anger.

"What errors?" I ask. Even though I can see the darkness fighting its way out, I'm not afraid. I let his darkness, his anger, surround me like a shield. Keeping everyone out and keeping me safe.

Bear's looking over my shoulder not really focusing on anything. The storm in his eyes is much stronger than the one outside. "He hired a piss pore lackey. My boys caught him and rung out every bit of information he had. Including a small shipment of women he plans to sell in four days."

Oh my gosh.

"What's reason number two?"

Bear stares into my eyes. He's searching so deep that there's no way I can hide the fact that I'm falling in love with him.

"He fucking touched what's mine."

# Chapter Fifteen

*Bear*

Watching Rose sleep helps calm the storm inside me. I didn't mention that I made a trip to her father's house. Brian Pierce's office was trashed. Whoever it was that killed Pierce was looking for something. I'm positive that something is my woman.

No matter how long I lay here watching her chest rise and fall, I can't get the image of that fucking basement room with the red door out of my head. What did she say Pierce called it? The Punishment room?

I would give anything to have that man alive and in front of me. Shot in his fucking sleep. The man deserved much more pain. I'll never have the satisfaction of watching his life drain from his eyes.

There was a metal operating table right in the center of that room. Chains hanging from the ceiling, on the floor, on the walls. I couldn't help the images that forced their way into my brain. My sweet Rose chained up while she was tortured by the one man who was supposed to protect and love her.

I'm pulled away from my thoughts when I hear my phone buzzing. Grabbing it from the bedside table, I quietly leave the room and shut the door before answering.

"Yeah."

"Prez, you need to get your woman over here as soon as fucking possible," I tense at the urgency in Chains` voice.

"Why?"

"I just got word that Hernández knows where Rose is and is making plans to grab her."

Over my dead fucking body. "Call everyone in. We're going into lockdown in one hour."

"Do you think it's necessary to call in everyone?" Chains asks. I understand where he's coming from, but I know what a desperate man will do to get a woman like Rose.

"Hernández has this stupid idea that Rose belongs to him. He's desperate and will do anything, go through anyone, to get her. Lockdown in one hour." I hang up before Chains has a chance to respond.

Taking a deep breath, I head toward my room. I open the door and can't help but chuckle. Rose is laying on her back with her legs spread apart and her hands above her head, trying to take up as much bed as her little body can. She looks like cute little starfish.

I sit on the side of the bed and push the hair off her face. God, she is so fucking beautiful. Every time I look at her, I get hard. I've jacked off more times since she's been here then I have in years. I could have found my release in any of the club girls, but the thought was only fleeting.

If Rose is willing, I want to give this, us, a try. I've never been in love before, but as it turns out when I fall, I fall hard. And, the second she's ready, I'll be burying my cock in her sweet pussy. I can't fucking wait.

I push those thoughts to the back of my mind for now. Leaning over, I grab onto Rose's hip and give it a few taps.

"Rose, baby, you need to get up. We have to go."

"Hmm? Huh? Go? Where do we have to go in the middle of the night?"

"I'll tell you everything when we get there. For now, I need you to quickly get dressed and pack anything you'll need for a few days."

Even though she's confused, she still nods her head and hops out of bed to do what I asked. She trusts me, and that feels fucking fantastic. Once she has everything packed, I grab her bag and head toward the door.

"What about your things? Am I going somewhere alone?" Her confusion has morphed into fear. I'm having none of that. Dropping her bag, I turn and gently hold her face between my hands.

"We're going to the clubhouse for a few days. I already have everything I need there." At her nod, I lean forward to kiss her forehead before grabbing her bag and hand and head out the door.

We arrive at the clubhouse roughly fifteen minutes later to utter chaos.

"Finally," Hawk yells as he runs toward us.

"What the hell is going on?" I ask him.

"We need to get Rose inside. There's some man here who is demanding to see her."

Without another word, I throw Hawk the duffel bag, lift Rose up bridal style and rush toward the building.

"HEY, WHAT ARE YOU DOING WITH MY SISTER?"

I hear Rose gasp as my steps falter. Sister?

"It's okay, Bear. That's my half-brother I was telling you about. Remember? The one who snuck me in the chocolate bars?"

I do remember her talking about him, but I trust him about as much as I trust Hernández.

"Please," she whispers. "He was the only person who was ever kind to me."

Seeing the sadness on her face pisses me off. Knowing the lack of kindness this woman has had in her life makes me want to scream. With a resigned sigh, I lower her to her feet and turn around. Keeping Rose behind me.

"Who are you?" I ask trying to give a bored vibe.

"My name is Josh Pierce. I'm her brother."

Already knowing his answer, I ask, "Whose brother?"

I watch as something, guilt perhaps, crosses his face before he answers, "Um, the ladies. The one behind your back."

"You say you're her brother, yet you can't tell me her name?" I know I'm just pushing here, but fuck, it pisses me off how she was treated.

"I do know her name. It just isn't one she's ever heard. Look, can I please talk to her? I just want to make sure she's okay. I also have something really important she needs to know."

Before I can tell this mother fucker exactly how I feel about him, Rose moves from behind my back and steps forward.

"Hello, Josh! How are you?" she asks in a small voice.

Everything in me wants to pick her back up and run her to safety. It takes every ounce of self-control I have to place my hand on her back and just wait.

"Hello, sister! Are you well?" The pompous ass actually looks like he cares.

"I'm doing well, brother. I hope it's not rude of me to ask, but what are you doing here?" The way Rose has reverted to the timid voice she had when I first met her has me furious.

"I thought you weren't afraid?" I whisper in her ear.

She turns her head slightly before answering, "I'm not."

"You sure sound like it."

"Force of habit, I guess," she shrugs.

"Father wouldn't allow us to speak. When we found

those rare occasions when we thought we were alone, whispering was always our best bet. Father caught us a couple of times and we were punished. I wasn't allowed back for many months," Josh speaks while looking at Rose.

"How were you punished?" Trigger asks.

Josh looks shocked at hearing Trigger speak. If it wasn't for his large presence, half the time you wouldn't even notice he was in the room. I'm not as surprised that he stepped forward.

Since the moment we all stepped into that damn room in Pierce's basement, they had questions. I told them everything that piece of shit inflicted on Rose. I even told them what Hernández did to her on her last day there. Trigger went through a similar experience with his kid brother.

"Umm..." Josh looks at Rose. Silently asking her for help. Moving my hand from her back to her hip, I just stare at Josh waiting for his answer. "Well, as I said, I would be banned from the house for a few months. He knew I loved coming there as often as I could. He just didn't know why."

"You got banned from the house?" Trigger says quietly. "Do you have any idea what your deadbeat father did to your sister?"

"No, that's why I've been going over more often. She has been withdrawn and scared since she was a little girl, but I never knew why. Every time I went, she was less and less a person, and more a shadow. Last year I got this letter in the mail asking for my help. I knew then that something more sinister was going on in that house when I was away."

Rose let out a soft sob before taking another step

closer to Josh. "Every time you came over, Father left me alone. He made me stay in my room or help his workers clean and cook. I didn't mind. You coming over were my favorite days."

Josh's face paled before he asked, "What did he do when I wasn't there?"

Not wanting Rose to relive that again, I ask if Josh wanted to come inside so we can talk. On the walk in he informed me that he knew his father was dead. He also told me he knew who put the hit out on his father. He just didn't know why.

Once inside, I walked Rose straight up to our room. Our room with the brand-new bed.

"I'm going to go talk to Josh for a little while. In the meantime, make yourself at home. Soon a lot of people will be here. I'll explain everything when I return."

"Bear."

"I won't be long,"

"Bear, I'm coming with you," she demanded.

"Sweetheart, your brother and I are going to have a heart to heart about a few things and it might be best if you didn't hear."

"You're going to tell him what Father did to me." Rose squared her shoulders and glared right into my eyes. "I have every right to be there. I can give him more detail that you can. I'm afraid, yes. There isn't a single moment when I'm not afraid. But, I'm strong enough to handle a freaking conversation, Landon Bear Allington!"

I stare at Rose with what I know is a shocked look. Look who is coming out of her shell.

"Who told you my real name?"

Rose's eyes widen and her face is heated with that beautiful blush. She's shocked herself with her little outburst.

"Um, I heard your mother call you by your first and last name. And, Hawk mentioned once that Bear and Hawk were your actual middle names."

"Yeah, my parents went a little wild with our names."

"I think they are beautiful. Bears are very protective, extremely curious, and insanely strong. Did you know that a brown Bear can crush a bowling ball with the force of its bite?" Smiling, I shake my head. "Hawks are one of the most intelligent birds and are extremely fast. Researchers have recorded some Hawks flying at almost two-hundred miles per hour during a hunt."

My grin stretched so far that my face actually hurt. "Where did you learn such fascinating facts?"

"Oh, um. I've read a lot of books."

Chuckling, I wrap her in my arms. "Alright, miss information. You can come with me. But the moment you start feeling overwhelmed we are out of there."

# Chapter Sixteen

*Rose*

We walk into Bears office and see Hawk, Trigger, Chains and Josh all waiting. Bear walks over to his desk and sits down in the well-used chair, pulling me onto his lap.

"Let's make this quick. Everyone is starting to show up."

"Okay," Josh takes a deep breath before continuing. "Do you remember how Father acted last Christmas, sister?"

"Uhm, I remember him being home more. I remember him whistling all the time. I guess you could say he was in a good mood." I think back to last Christmas and picture my father walking about the halls and whistling tunes. He didn't talk to me much, but that was when he started giving me those creepy looks. The ones that made me feel uncomfortable.

"Yes, he had just received news that a deal he had been working on was going to pull through. He never told me what that deal was. I did find out who it was with shortly after." I nod my head because I already have an idea on who he's talking about. "So, right after Christmas, I got a letter in the mail from a woman named, Sandra Brown. Have you ever heard of her?"

"No," I whisper. I don't know why, but my body starts to shake. It's like it's already reacting to some big news Josh is about to deliver. I feel Bears arms tighten around me.

"I have the letter here. It might be easier if I just let you read it instead of me trying to explain it to you."

Josh reaches into his pocket, pulls out a white envelope and slides it across Bear's desk. I stare at it for what feels like hours before Bear reaches over and picks it up. I can't find it in me to open the letter. I just have this feeling my whole world is about to change. Again.

With one arm still wrapped around me, Bear somehow opens and unfold the letter. He holds it right where we both can read it. Taking a deep breath, I lean further into the protection that is Bear and silently follow along while he reads aloud for all of us.

*Dear Josh,*

*You don't know me, but I desperately need your help. My name is Sandra Brown, and Twenty-Five years ago I made a terrible mistake. You see, I was a drug addict. The only thought on my mind was how I would get my next fix. When you're in that position, you will do anything, and I mean anything, to get what you desperately crave.*

*I've been watching you, Josh. I'm pretty sure you're a good person. Nothing like your father. Your father is NOT a good man. No matter what he lets the world see. I know this because I used to be his best friend. We used to be inseparable. We had a child together, but still, the only thing I could think about was my next fix.*

*He kept demanding that I sign over all my rights to our daughter and walk away. I couldn't do it. But then he stopped giving me money and I couldn't get what I needed. So, I did what was best for me. I signed the papers, I got my money and I walked away from my perfect, beautiful little girl.*

*I left my angel with that monster.*

*I have a source from inside Brian's house that tells me she is being mistreated in the most terrible ways. That she is not living life but is merely surviving. I'm told that Brian has major plans for her involving a man named Roman Hernández. Something that will better his life but could very well end hers. I don't know what those plans are. I don't know when they will take place. But, please, get my daughter out of there before anything happens.*

*Find someone to protect my Amara. Someone who can protect her with their life. Tell her I love her with everything I am. Tell her that I am so sorry I took so long to straighten myself out and rescue her from the prison I signed her up for. I hope one day she can find it in her heart to forgive me.*

*Sandra Brown*

Bear places the letter on his desk and wraps both arms around me. Holding me tightly as if I might fall apart at any moment. Which is exactly how I feel. The tears are clouding my vision and I'm trying my best to hold it together.

"These came with the letter," Josh places a piece of paper and a picture on the desk in front of us.

"Baby," Bear gently turns my head toward him and wipes away my fallen tears. "My sweet girl."

"No one has ever wanted me, Bear." The feeling of betrayal from a mother I never knew goes deep, I can feel it in my very soul.

"That just simply isn't true, my girl. I want you more than I want my next breath." Bear holds my face hostage against his gaze. "I want you in my life for the rest of our days, baby. I want you in my house, I want you wearing my patch, swollen with my children. I want you forever by my side."

It's so hard to think with Bear this close. His scent of sandalwood and motor oil invade my nose. I feel his hard body as I sit on his lap, his rough but protective arm wrapped around my waist and the firm grip he has on my chin.

On top of that sensory overload, I'm trying to process his words. He's told me before that I was his. I don't think he understands what being with me would entail. I want him. God, do I want him. He makes me feel safe, wanted… loved. I'm not saying he loves me in that way, but I still feel loved in some small way.

I don't think I will ever truly be loved, though. Not the kind of love that I've come to understand.

The kind of love I have for Bear.

"There's so much about me that needs to be changed, Bear. I'm not a normal woman. I'm shy. I'm afraid of this new world. Why would you want to be with someone like me? Someone who needs more help than most children?" I close my eyes to get away from his stare.

"Eye's baby," he demands. I give it a few more seconds to collect myself before doing as he asks. I expect him to be angry, but his eyes are soft and full of something I don't quite understand. "First off, you being shy and afraid of this world isn't something you can control. We will work on it…together. But, you gotta know sweetheart, there isn't a damn thing I would change about you."

"Oh, okay," I stupidly say. Because what does a girl say to that?

"Well, maybe there is one thing I would change," he says, with a cocky grin.

"What's that?" I whisper.

"Your last name. Allington sounds a hell of a lot better than Pierce. Don't you think?"

He lets go of my shocked face with a chuckle. What

does that mean? Does he want me to be his wife, one day?

Oh my!

I turn back to the table and the small group of people I momentarily forgot were in the room. Picking up the paper I see that it's a birth certificate. My birth certificate.

"Amara Rosalie Pierce," I say under my breath.

"Amara is such a beautiful name, baby." Bear is massaging the back of my neck while looking over my shoulder.

I nod my head because I agree. It is. However...

"It is a pretty name, but it doesn't feel like it's mine. I like being your Rose." I feel my face heating up with embarrassment at my admission.

"You will always, and forever be my Rose." The look in his eyes has me believing every word. "Besides, did you see your middle name?"

"Rosalie," I say under my breath.

"That's right. Amara Rosalie. You were always meant to be my sweet, beautiful Rose."

Someone clears their throat, so I focus back on the desk and grab the picture. The second my brain recognizes who I'm seeing everything starts slowly fading.

"Bear, that's him," I said in a panic. "That's the man my father sold me to. That's Roman Hernández."

I don't hear or see anyone's reaction because the next second everything faded away and I was surrounded by darkness.

# Chapter Seventeen

*Bear*

Standing with Rose in my arms, I head toward the door.

"Chains, I want that motherfucker found. I want him and that whole fucking cartel taken down, and I want it done yesterday."

"Is my sister okay?"

"She's fine," I hear Hawk say. "A person can only handle so much before they shut down. She just needs some time to rest and process everything."

Not wanting or caring what anyone else has to say, I make my way back up to our room. The clubhouse is packed, and I know I will need to take a minute and explain to everyone why they're here. It makes for much less chaotic situations if you let the family members in on enough detail to keep them alert.

Halfway up the stairs, Rose opens her eyes.

"Oh, how embarrassing. I keep passing out in front of you." Rose fidgets, but instead of trying to get down she snuggles into my body and rests her head in the crease of my neck.

Mine.

"We didn't even get a chance to tell Josh what was happening to me."

"Trigger and Hawk know enough to fill him in. I just want you to rest."

Once in our room, I gently lay her on our bed and smooth her hair out of her face.

"I have to run downstairs for a few minutes to explain

to everyone what's going on and I'll be right back." I hate leaving her, but the sooner I get this over with the sooner I can get back to her.

"What exactly is going on, Bear?"

Shit. I was hoping to let her rest before I slam her with even more bad news.

"We got word that Roman Hernández found out where you were and is planning to make an attempt to grab you."

I can see the emotions play out on her face. Fear, acceptance, anger. But, the one that surprises me the most was grim determination.

"Tell me what to do."

"What do you mean?"

"You can use me, Bear. You told me that you were trying to find a way to stop whatever it is that he's doing. I don't really understand why he wants me, and I'm so freaking scared, but wouldn't it be easier to get him to come to you?"

"Absolutely fucking not! We are not using you as bait, Rose. We have our plans on how to take that bastard down and putting you anywhere near his sight is not even in the realm of possibilities."

"But…"

"No."

"Fine," she sighs. "So, somehow, he found out where I was and he's on his way here? What I don't understand is why you would bring all these people here if there's a chance this guy will show up at any moment? Even if he thinks I'm at your cabin he will eventually put two and two together."

"I bring everyone in as a safety measure. Yeah, he's going to find out that you're here. If he doesn't already know. It's better to have everyone safe in one place then it is having them all spread apart. This way, the brothers can keep an eye on everyone at once. You never know what a man like Hernández will do to get what he wants."

Her eyes grow wide with fear. I hate that look on her face. I will stop the world if I have to in order to make it go away.

"What if he hurts someone anyway? What if he finds a way inside and hurts someone because of me?"

Oh, the fear wasn't for her. It was for everyone else.

"I'm so tired of playing the victim, Bear. I'm so tired of being afraid. I just want to be happy." She pushes herself up to sit on the bed. "Yes, I'm ignorant about the world. I have no clue how to survive on my own. But I am no longer a victim. You said I was yours. Is that true?" She says the last words so quietly I almost didn't catch them.

Reaching out and taking her hands, I hold her gaze so she can read the truth in my eyes. "Yes, you are mine with everything you are. Just as I am yours with everything I am."

Rose gives me that beautiful smile as a single tear trails down her cheek. I lean in and kiss the tear away. A happy tear. My happy tear. Never going to waste those happy tears.

"Then I will stand proudly at your side. I will lean on your strength and trust your judgments. I will give you my heart in the hope that one day I can have a piece of yours as well."

Silly woman. "Don't you see it?"

With a confused look, she asks, "See what?"

Chuckling, I lift her hand and place it on my chest. Directly over my heart. "You can never have a piece of my heart, Rose." At her look, I hurry to finish. "You can't have a piece, because you already own the whole thing. I am wholly yours, sweetheart. You own me, heart and soul."

Rose hops up onto her knees and stares down at me. "Wait," she says. She pauses and just looks into my eyes. Deeper than she ever has before. Understanding what she's looking for, I let it all show. Every last bit of love I have for her is right there for her to see.

"You love me?" She asks. I don't give her a verbal answer. I wait for her to fully grasp what she's seeing.

"Oh god, you love me."

"Yeah, she's finally getting it," I say right before I grab the back of her head and slam my lips onto hers. I only let myself have a small sip before I reluctantly move back.

I stand up and gently place Rose on her feet. "Let's head downstairs."

I reach the door before she speaks up, "Bear, I love you, too. So very much."

"I know, baby. I can see it shining in your eyes."

****Rose****

***It's been a*** few days since Bear issued a lockdown. He did explain to everyone who I was and what was going down with Roman Hernández. He gave them just enough detail to be on the lookout without them knowing too much.

My brother decided to stay until Hernández was no longer a threat. That didn't go down well with Trigger. Apparently, Josh is Trigger's least favorite person at the moment. For reasons, I don't quite understand.

There are a ton of people here. No matter where I look, there's always someone there. It's not really a bad thing,

I'm just not used to being around so many people. It's emotionally exhausting, to be honest.

Bear is usually in meetings or outside on watch duty most of the time. So, I don't get to see him much during the day. But every night he climbs into bed behind me kisses my shoulder and holds me tight against him for the rest of the night.

One night after he pulled me to him, I could feel his hardness against my back. I know about intercourse. I know what that hardness meant. I also know the first time is said to be painful. With that thought in my mind, I tensed up. Bear must have felt it because he tightens his hold on me and whispered in my ear, "When you're ready, baby. Not a second before."

"How will we know when I'm ready?" I whispered back.

"At that moment, we'll both feel it," was his answer.

I also got to know Princess and Ma better. It was nice spending time with the two females. Today we were in the kitchen cooking the largest pot of chili I have ever seen. Well, Ma was cooking it. She kind of took over when Princess and I weren't preparing it the way she wanted.

"What are you ladies up to?" Hawk asks as he sits beside Princess.

"We've been booted by Ma," Princess answers him. "Apparently we weren't mixing the chili 'deep enough' and were fired as Sous chefs."

"Hawk, wheels up in five," Bear says from behind me.

Smiling, I turn around and look up. "Hey there, handsome."

"Well, hello beautiful," he says with a chuckle before leaning down and gently kissing my lips. Looking in the kitchen he says, "Ma, what smells so good."

"That would be chili, dear boy. You going to be back in time to get a bowl before it's all gone?"

"Should be," he says before looking down at me. "I have to go take care of something. I should only be gone for a few hours. I need you to promise me you won't leave this building. Not for anything."

"Of course. I'll stay right here with Ma and Princess until I'm ready for bed."

The thought of him leaving is causing my heart to beat faster but I also know I can't stay glued to him for the rest of my life.

"I'll be fine, honey. Go do whatever it is you have to do. I'll be waiting for you when you get back."

Bear lets out a low growl. "I find that I love it when you call me honey. Do it again. Do it always, my love."

I smile shyly at him as he reaches in for one last kiss before turning and walking to where Hawk, Trigger, and Chains are all waiting for him.

"Girls, I'm going to go ahead and turn in for the night. Finish up this chili and make sure the kids eat first," Ma says.

"Are you sure you trust us with your soup, Ma? I might end up serving it with the wrong hand or something," Princess teases.

"Oh, hush you silly thing. Goodnight ladies."

"Goodnight, Ma. I hope you sleep sweet," I tell her.

"Let's get everyone fed so we can go be lazy and watch a movie," Princess says.

I stand up with a smile and help serve chili.

# Chapter Eighteen

*Bear*

That fucking package. Why the hell did I wait so long to open it? If Hawk hadn't asked about it this morning it would have sat in my desk drawer for who knows how long.

"So, tell me again why we have to leave so quickly," Chains said as we were walking out of the clubhouse.

"That package had a USB drive inside," I told the brothers around me. "Someone sent me blueprints of Hernández's compound."

"Who would be brave enough to do something that stupid?" Chains wondered.

"Not sure. There was also a small list of dates and times of events that Hernández would be away at. We can't just sit on this information. So, we're heading into the city to meet up with Detective Dick."

Detective Rick Anderson is the head honcho on the Hernández case. He's also a massive dick. It takes everything I have not to strangle him every time he opens his mouth.

"Fucking dick," murmurs Hawk.

I love my brother.

I hop on my Harley and lead the way to Detective Dick's office.

***

***"So, tell me*** where you got this information," Dick demands.

"It was delivered a little over a week ago. I had too much shit on my mind to open a damn package, so I tossed in a drawer and forgot about it until a few hours ago."

"You've been sitting on this for over a week? We could have already taken the bastard down had I had this sooner."

Dick.

"You have it now. There's information on there that puts him at his father's estate tomorrow evening. I want this done by the books so none of my men are blamed and put behind bars."

"It's probably best if you just sit this one out."

"I don't fucking think so," Trigger growls.

"Not happening. We have personal involvement in this now. Either you let us help or we do it on our own," I inform him.

Detective Dick acquiesced with a nod. Not that I needed his approval. Hernández is after my woman and I will stop at nothing to make him gone.

"Alright, but we do this my way. I don't need Hernández tipped off before we even get close because he hears a bunch of damn bikes roaring down the road."

"We're not fucking stupid."

"Hawk, I got it," I tell my twin. "First and foremost, don't disrespect my men again. You forget, detective, who keeps this town clean? Do you forget who keeps the gangs out? Who helps you with the cases that need someone to go a bit further than the law allows? The Infernal sons deserve your respect, and you will give it."

I pause, giving Detective Dick a moment to really hear my words.

"Now, we will follow your lead, but if I get to Hernández first, I make no promises."

"I guess that will have to work. Pack your boys up. I'll meet you at your club in one hour."

With nothing left to say, we all stand and head outside to our bikes. I need to get back to my ol' lady.

# Chapter Nineteen

*Rose*

I woke with a start. At first, I thought it was from a dream, but I remember my dream. I remember exactly what I was doing when I woke up. Just washing the dishes in Bear's cabin. Weird I know, but it's a nice reprieve from my normal nightmares.

No, something else caused me to wake so suddenly.

Wait, what's that smell?

BANG! BANG! BANG!

I jump from my bed at the sound of someone banging on my door. Shaking my head, I wrap the blanket around me and walk over to see who it is. I'm about to touch the handle when I notice the smoke coming in the room from beneath the door. Is the building on fire? Grabbing the edge of the blanket, I grab onto to the handle and swing the door wide open.

That's when I knew I made a terrible mistake.

Turning, I try to run back into the room. I don't get more than a few steps before I'm hit over the back of the head. The only thing I see as everything fades to black are the cold eyes and sinister smile…

Of Roman Hernández.

# Chapter Twenty

*Bear*

We arrive back to utter chaos. The building is in flames, people are running around screaming and crying. Firefighters are racing to beat back the fire eating away at our sacred clubhouse.

None of that matters. I have only one thought.

Where is Rose?

"What the fuck happened?" Hawk asks.

"Listen up. Hawk, I need you to do a headcount. Check and make sure everyone got out safely. Trigger, I need you to round up all the brothers. Have them escort their family's home and then meet back here." I turn and walk right toward the firemen. I need answers and I need my woman. Not in that order.

"I can talk to them, brother. You go look for your ol' Lady," Chains says from right beside me.

"Sounds good to me. Come find me if you find anything out."

Clapping Chains on the shoulder, I turn around and scan the crowd. Rose is so tiny she could be anywhere. I spend the next ten minutes searching but can't find her. My heart is doing double time. If she isn't out here, then she's still in the building.

I do the only logical thing. I run straight for the fire.

"Bear, what the fuck?" is said right before someone slams me down on the ground.

"SHE'S IN THERE. SHE'S STILL IN THE FUCKING BUILDING. LET ME GO. I HAVE TO SAVE HER."

"Listen to me, Prez. She's not in there. There's no one else in the building. They've searched it thoroughly and said everyone got out safely."

That news calms me down. But, not by much.

"Then where is she, Chains? I've looked everywhere. She isn't out here. If she isn't out here, or in there then, where is she?"

"I think I have an idea."

I nudge Chains off my back and jump to my feet. Standing in front of us is Slim with a grim look on his face.

"Slim, what do you know? What are you even doing here?"

"So, I've been keeping my eyes and ears on Carrie. When you kicked her out, she went straight home and sulked for a few days. But then she made one phone call. This was before I was able to tap into her cell, so at the time, I had no idea who she called." Whatever he has to say next, I can tell I will not like it.

"When she left, I followed her. Straight to Roman Hernández's territory." That fucking bitch. I knew I should have killed her. "I couldn't stay too long, but I did stay long enough to see something that you might find interesting. Carrie was meeting Hernández at some dive bar. About ten minutes into their meeting, fucking Derrick sat down with them."

"Derrick?" Chains asks. "As in hang-around Derrick?"

"The very same."

"This is fucking bad, brother."

"Yeah, it is. Let's go find Hawk."

"Oh, he's by his truck with Trigger. I have a little surprise for you," Slim says as he walks towards Hawk's truck.

We arrive to see Trigger sitting in the back of the

truck…using a struggling Derrick as an ass cushion.

"Bear, did you find Rose?" Hawk asks.

"No, and I've looked everywhere. The firefighters told Chains that there wasn't a single soul in the building. But I have a feeling Derrick here might be able to help us find her."

"That's not the only thing, brother."

At Hawks tone, I look away from Derricks red face to my brothers very pissed off one.

"Princess. She's gone, too."

We all stand in stunned silence. My little princess and my beautiful Rose are both gone. And, I have a feeling they are in the hands of evil.

"Trigger, I want answers. And I want them fast."

"Not a single problem. Meet me at your cabin in twenty minutes," he tells me. "By the time you get there, I'll have all the information he has to give."

"I'll drive," Hawk says. He walks up to me and touches his forehead to mine. "We will find them both. And, when we do and we get them safe, there will be nothing left of Roman Hernández for Detective Dick to find."

Borrowing some of my brother's strength, because mine has been scared out of me, I stand up straight and get this shit with the firefighters done with so they can leave. My building isn't completely gone, but I don't give a fuck if it falls to the ground in a pile of ash.

I have only two objectives in my mind. Get my ol' lady and Princess back and then…

Revenge.

Forty-five minutes later I pull into my driveway. Trigger, Chains, Hawk, Slim, Brick, and Josh are all sitting on my porch. I see Derrick's dead body in the back of Hawks truck.

"What are you doing here?" I ask Josh.

"I won't let her down again," was all he said. Good enough for me.

A quick look in Trigger's eyes and I know we have some good information.

"So, Carrie was the rat. She was delivering those recordings to Hernández in exchange for a fuck ton of money," Trigger snarls.

"Apparently, she dug her way into his life as deep as she could go so that she could get information on him to give to you. She was trying to bribe you for ol' lady status," Brick narrowed his eyes as he spoke. "She was a fucking lunatic."

"Was?"

"Oh, I didn't tell you the best part. She was the one who sent the package. I guess she was afraid we were going to catch her, and she figured this would earn her protection. Hernández found out and killed her."

"Doesn't matter," Trigger cuts in. "We got the information we needed. Let's go get our girls back," he says with a knowing grin.

I let it slide this time, but not without glaring at the man.

Hold on, baby. Stay strong for me. I'm coming.

# Chapter Twenty-One

*Rose*

"Hey, wake up?"

My goodness, my head is pounding. What did I get hit with?

"Are you okay?" A familiar voice asks.

"Where am I?"

"We're in some type of cargo container, I think. How did they get you out without anyone seeing? I tried to warn you. I knew something was wrong the moment I smelled smoke."

"Who are you?" I ask. I'm confused and having a hard time focusing. Taking a fortifying breath, I finally open my eyes.

"Rose, it's me, Princess."

"What?" I swing my head in her direction just as the cargo doors open.

"Well, well, well. Look what we have here. My bride and a side toy. Must be my lucky day. I've been looking everywhere for you, bride. Let's go. Time to go home."

"We're not going anywhere with you, fucker," yells Princess.

Before my next blink, Roman has Princess by the hair jerking her head back.

"You know what, bride, I think I'll play with my toy first." He shoves Princess against the side of the container.

"No, please stop," I beg him. "Please, just leave her alone. Let her go and I'll come with you."

"Oh, you'll be coming with me regardless. However, I think I did just find a way to make you cooperate." Roman release Princess and she falls to the floor curling into herself. I've never seen her look so defeated.

"Both of you, get the fuck out here now or so help me god, bride, I will fuck your friend in every hole she has and force you to watch," Roman says from outside the container.

Knowing he's not lying I walk over to Princess and help her stand. "Come on, honey."

"Rose, I'm scared."

"I know, Princess. I am, too. We must try and stay strong. Bear will come for us. You and I both know he will."

I just hope he isn't too late when he does, Rose silently thought.

***

***We don't travel*** long before we stop in front of a large two-story white house. The front door swings open and an older gentleman walks out heading straight for us. He is the spitting image of Roman. Must be his father.

"Mijo, what took you so long? I was about to send out Benny," the older man greets when Roman opens the car door.

"I don't need Benny to fucking babysit me, papa," he says as he exits the car, leaving the door open. "I ran into a little snag. Tonio took care of it."

"What was your *snag,* mijo?"

"A bitch. She was trying to warn the woman of my arrival before I had a chance to announce it myself."

I give Princess a squeeze. We're still sitting in the car

while they talk. I'm looking around trying to find a way out. Maybe when they aren't looking, we can make a run for it. It's worked for me once before.

"Where is Tonio?"

"He's pulling up now. He had a stop to make. Said he was hungry. Pendejo"

Just then someone pulls in behind us.

"Hola amigos. Where is my pretty prize?"

The car door opens, and Princess is ripped out of my arms. I follow behind her and see a man dragging her toward the house.

"ROSE, PLEASE HELP ME."

Running as fast as I can to reach them, I hit the man's back with as much force as I can. It's not long before I'm lifted and thrown back into a flowerbed hitting my head with enough force to cause my vision to blank out for a few seconds.

"Please," I whimpered. "I said I would do everything you say. Please, don't hurt her."

"Oh, I have no plans on hurting her. Tonio here, however, is another story. He enjoys his women in pain." Roman is still standing back with his father near the car just watching everything happen.

I act before I think. I grab the nearest rock and run for the one called Tonio. He's bent over trying to pick Princess up where she's curled herself into a ball. I raise my arm back and hit him as hard as I can in the back of the head.

I know I'm not that strong, but adrenaline must be on my side because Tonio drops to the ground. Reaching down, I grab Princess's hand.

"Let's go," I whisper. "Run."

I don't know what made me think we even had a

chance knowing that Roman and his father, and probably this Benny character, were watching us, but I knew that we weren't going down without a fight.

We run toward the tree line. We almost make it when a loud bang sounds out. Princess's hand drops from mine and I turn to grab it again. Not feeling her, I turn around. That's when I notice she's fallen. I rush to her, slamming down on my knees. She's looking up at the sky with tears in her eyes. A single tear slides down her face and lands in the growing puddle beneath her.

She flicks her gaze to me, and her lips tip into a small smile as I watch the last bit of life leave her eyes.

I don't fight as I'm lifted from her still body and thrown across someone's shoulder. I don't fight when we enter a building that must have been hidden behind the house. I don't fight when they chain me by my hands and lift my arms above my head. I don't fight when my nightgown is ripped from my body and I'm left alone and naked in the dark room.

I don't fight because Princess is dead, and I know with everything I am that it's my fault. I deserve whatever they have planned for me. Bear can't save me now. No one can.

# Chapter Twenty-Two

*Bear*

It's been six hours. Six fucking hours. Derrick gave Trigger five locations where they could have taken Rose and Princess.

The first three, two warehouses and an old boathouse, weren't a complete bust but there were no signs of the women. We found nothing of value in the first warehouse but there were crates of drugs and guns in the other one. The boathouse had four frightened women locked in the only bedroom room. None of which spoke English. These must be the women Hernández planned to sell.

I had no choice but to call in detective Dick. Now, he thinks he's taking point for the next two locations. A cargo container about half an hour away and Hernández's childhood home.

Well, fuck that.

"I don't give a single fuck what your laws say. My girls are missing, and I will get them back."

"And, I will help you get them back. But we finally have everything we need to put Hernández in a cage for the rest of his miserable life and I will not have that ruined by a bunch of cavemen out for revenge."

I know what he says makes sense, but I can't see past the red haze that has taken over my vision since discovering Rose was taken.

"Chains," I say to my VP.

He takes a few seconds to read me before nodding. "I got it."

"How about we split into teams," Chains suggests to

the detective. "You can lead the first one and another of your detectives heads the second. We'll split the brothers up between the two and then hit both places at once."

"Sounds reasonable enough," Bear says. "Chains, Ink, Slim and Brick, you all go with the second team. Hawk, Trigger, and Josh, you come with me."

"Detective Hudson, you're with them," he gestures to Chains. "Head to the Hernández estate. We'll take the cargo container. Make sure you grab those search warrants. Everything by the book. I want no fuck-ups."

"You got it," the detective replies.

Without another word, we all head out the door.

****Rose****

***You think I*** would be used to pain. Having my arms tied above my head isn't all that new. But, it's different now. Roman somehow pulled me higher when he chained me up, giving me just enough room to stand on my toes.

I'm standing as high as I can on the tip of my toes trying to relieve the fire in my shoulders. Every now and again, my knees go weak and my legs give out. Each time that happens the pain in my shoulders is so severe that I almost faint.

The pain, I can deal with. However, I'm completely naked and it's freezing in here. If I don't do something soon, I'm going to die of hyperthermia. I'm trying to remember what the signs of hyperthermia are when the door opens, and the room is flooded with a cold wind.

"Hello, bride," Roman says while flipping on a light. "In the morning you will become my wife. Then we'll be heading home where we can consummate our marriage for as long as we wish."

Is he crazy? He's just talking like this is a very typical conversation that we've had many times before. Like I'm not tied up like an animal waiting to be butchered. He almost sounds...bored.

"I will never marry you," I tell him through shivering teeth. "I will never willingly go to your bed. I'd rather die."

"Now, now. Be careful what you say. I do so enjoy a challenge. However, you belong to me. Your father made a deal with mine over twenty years ago, that in exchange for Hernández support during an election of his choosing, I get you. Well, as you can see, I got you, but your father got dead. Papa didn't want him as governor."

"You killed my friend," I scream, ignoring the bit about my father. I'm not shocked in the slightest. "I will never stop fighting you. The first time you turn your back on me, I will shove a knife right in it. Literally or metaphorically. I will never truly be yours."

Something flickers behind Roman's eyes, but it's gone before I can guess what it was.

"Benny killed your friend. But I did kill your father. Went back the next morning to collect my bride and learned that while I was away, she escaped. His execution was already planned, I just saved my family the time and money, is all."

I don't know if he was expecting me to be shocked by this information or if he was trying to make me break. What he doesn't know is, I don't really care. My life is better without that good for nothing man in it. He did me a favor.

"So," he continues. "Here's what we're going to do.

I'm going to let you down. Then we will go inside, get cleaned up and go to bed. We have a rather eventful day tomorrow."

He's lost his mind.

"The second you turn your back," I remind him.

The calm expression he's been wearing since coming into the building vanishes and in its place is pure rage.

"I will have nothing but your complete obedience, woman," he says in a terrifyingly calm voice.

I'm the most scared as I have ever been, but I can't let him beat me. My body yes, but he will never get my mind.

"The very second," I whisper just one more time.

The chain holding me is jerked and my body is lifted completely off the ground.

"Fight as hard as you want, little mouse. No one is coming for you. Everyone you ever cared about is dead. Including that Infernal Sons bastard. You're completely and utterly alone. Completely and utterly mine."

Bear's dead? I can feel my heart turning to ash with the thought alone.

A look of victory crosses Roman's face. He knew just what to say to break down my barrier.

"I think a few more hours hanging here will do you some good. Teach you some obedience that your father was supposed to have perfected by now."

Bear's dead. The overwhelming emotions that flood my body is this all-consuming vortex of agony, and if I don't let it out now, I'm going to burst. So, I do the only thing I can.

I scream. I scream with every bit of heartache I have. I kick out with my legs and manage a single blow to Roman's stomach. I wasn't actually trying to kick him. It just feels like my whole body is combusting.

“Still have a little fight left, I see,” Roman yells above my screaming before releasing the chain and turning around. “Well, just in case, we’ll do a little something to slow you down in case you manage to break free.”

I don’t fully acknowledge what he says. However, I understand his meaning a moment later when he swings a sledgehammer right against my left knee, and then my right. No longer able to hold myself up, my knees give out and I’m left hanging by my wrists alone.

It’s the worst physical pain I have ever been in. But nothing compares to the pain and emptiness in my heart.

I’m so sorry, my love.

My last thought is of Bear smiling down at me before I finally give in and slip into the waiting arms of darkness.

# Chapter Twenty-Three

*Bear*

"Detective, we pulled the security footage you asked for."

We found nothing inside the storage container, but Hawk did notice a camera pointing in its direction.

"Thank you, Mr. Smythe," Detective Dick, says. "Lead the way."

Mr. Smythe owns the shipping company that rented Hernández the storage container.

"We fast-forwarded it to the times you asked for," Mr. Smythe says, as we enter his office. "Well leave you to it, then. Come on Zack."

I have the video playing before the men even reach the door.

"Fast forward it at the slowest setting," Hawk says.

I do, and for a while, nothing happens. But then a red ford truck pulls up directly in front of the storage unit and I hit play. A man too big to be Hernández gets out and reaches back inside. Then he pulls out a struggling woman. Trigger reaches around and pauses the video right on her face.

"Princess," he growls.

"Keep going," the detective says.

Fucking dick.

We resume the video and watch as the man opens the door to the container and practically throws Princess inside before shutting the door back. Holding back my outburst, I continue watching.

A few minutes later another car pulls behind the truck. It's easy to tell who this is. Roman Hernández. He says something to the other man.

"What's that bastard saying? Does this thing have sound?" I question.

"It's video only," Mr. Smythe says as he re-enters the room.

Hernández says something else and the first man goes to the trunk of the car. The trunk opens and the man reaches in and lifts out a limp Rose.

"Goddammit!" I shout.

They take her to the same container Princess was thrown into. As soon as the door opens Princess darts right past the man and runs right into Hernández. He lifts her up and both men take the women in the container and leave a few seconds later.

"So, we know they were here," Hawk says. "Let's keep watching and find out when they left."

About an hour later, Hernández returns and enters where my girls are. A few minutes later, he exits with Rose and a scared Princess following behind and they all enter his car. What the fuck happened in there?

My phone buzzes in my pocket moments before the detective's rings. Seeing that it's Chains, I answer.

"Yeah."

"Prez, we've been here at the Hernández estate for about thirty minutes now. We can't get close enough to see anything, but we did just hear a fucking gun go off. We're going in. Get here fast, brother."

"Fuck, we're about ten minutes away... We'll be there in five."

I hang up and run back to the detective's car while explaining what the call was about. We all jump in and rush toward the estate going well over the speed limit.

A notch up for Detective Dick.

"Brother, I hate to say this, but you need to prepare for what we might find. We all need to prepare. They've been in his hands for almost ten hours now."

I don't say anything. The knot in my throat wouldn't let me even if I wanted to. I nod my acknowledgment and prepare myself for what's to come.

I do something that I don't ever remember doing, even as a young boy. I pray.

'Please Lord, let my girls be okay.'

***

***We arrive at*** the Hernández estate roughly four and a half minutes later to Chains and his team seconds away from barging into the building.

"You got here just in time, brother. We're just waiting for the all-clear from Detective Hudson," Chains says.

Detective Dick walks up to us while shoving his phone back in his pocket. "I called for backup and an ambulance. Just in case," he finishes when he sees my look.

His phone goes off. "Rick," he answers. "What do you have for me, Hudson?"

"Alright, take your team and form a perimeter around the house, we'll just simply go through the front door. Two minutes."

"Alright," he says as he turns his gaze on me. "Hudson has counted four men inside. Roman and his father being two of them. He hasn't seen any signs of the women since he arrived, but that doesn't really mean anything."

"Hernández is desperate for Rose," I growl out. "She

won't be far from his side."

"Hudson and his team are on every possible exit," the detective tells us. "I'll go in first with the warrant. Can't stress this enough, by the fucking book!!!!

"Buckle up boys," Chains says with a sinister grin. "It's ass-kicking time."

We all quietly make our way down the driveway. I have a couple of my guys stay with the other detectives to watch the exits. It's not that I don't trust them, even though I don't, but my woman's life is on the line. By the books or not, I'm getting her back.

Chains and Brick go around to the back exits. Smart brothers.

On the detective's mark, we burst through the door. It opens right into the living room where Hernández and his father are sitting on a couch.

"WHAT THE FUCK," shouts Hernández as he reaches behind him and pulls out a handgun.

He aims right for me and pulls the trigger. Before the bullet can connect, I'm shoved out of the way and the bullet lodges itself into Rick's shoulder.

Another notch up for the detective.

Trigger must see that Hernández is distracted by what just happened and he rushes forward, disarms him and shoves him down on the floor. At the same time, Ink does the same thing to Hernández's father.

I glance over at the detective to make sure he's still breathing before I jump up and head for Hernández.

"WHERE THE FUCK IS MY WOMAN?" I shout.

The sick fuck laughs and says, "You'll never find her."

Just then, a shot sounds out from somewhere in the house. I head toward the noise with the detective tight on my heels. We end up in a kitchen with a giant on the floor groaning.

"You shot me in the fucking ass. Damn, do you have no morals?" the man asks.

Looking over, I see Chains with a smirk on his face.

"Goddammit, Chains. What part of 'by the book' did you not get?" Detective Dick asks.

"Well, I did say freeze," the smart-ass replies.

"Where is my woman?" I ask the man.

"I don't fucking know who your woman is. Besides, there are no women in this house."

Brick comes into the kitchen shoving a man at gunpoint.

"I give up," the detective says, shaking his head.

"Hey, that's the man from the surveillance footage," Hawk says from behind me. "The one who had Princess in his truck."

"Tell him what he wants to know," Brick says to the man.

"Or what?" the man replies.

"Or I will pull every one of your mother fucking teeth out one by one," Trigger says from the doorway.

The man goes pale before he stammers out, "The building behind the house."

I don't wait for anyone to respond. I run to the nearest exit and rush outside. I find the small building in the back corner of the back yard.

As soon as my hand is on the handle, I yank the door open. The room is eerily quiet and dark.

I'm feeling around the walls trying to find a light switch.

"Rose, baby, are you in here?"

No response. I don't hear a single thing.

Finding a switch, I click it on, and the buildings single

room lights up. What I see steals my breath and nearly brings me to my knees. Rose is chained up, hanging by her wrists from the ceiling and completely naked.

And, she's not breathing.

"Holy fuck," someone says from behind me.

"Help me get her down," I tell anyone.

"Grab ahold of her body. Releasing the chain now."

Rose's limp body falls into my arms. She's so cold. Her lips are blue, lifeless.

"Get that fucking ambulance here now," someone shouts.

"There's no pulse," someone else shouts.

Laying Rose on the floor I give her all my breath. Every breath I inhale, I feed to her.

My brain comes back around and I rub her chest to try to get her heart to start.

I'm numb to the world around me. My full focus is on Rose.

"Come on baby, breath for me. You can't leave me now. I just got you," I plead.

After what feels like hours, but was most likely only a minute or two, Rose gasps a deep breath in. And that's the moment my heart started working again.

Rose is placed on a backboard and lifted onto a stretcher. I don't complain because I know she needs them more than she needs me at the moment. But, fuck it all if I let them go without me.

"Are you family?" One EMT asks as he's tucking a heated blanked around Rose.

"I'm her husband," I say, daring a single soul to deny me.

"I grab Rose's hand and ask the question I think I already know the answer to.

“Baby, where’s Princess?”

Her eyes are filled with so much sadness.

“Bear? I thought you were dead.”

“No, my sweet girl. I’m right here,” I lift her hand up and kiss her palm before placing her hand on my face, careful of her wrists.

“Where’s Princess, baby?”

“Oh, Bear,” she says as tears run down her face. “She’s dead. They killed her. I’m so very sorry.”

My heart breaks for my little princess. I’ll find out the details later. Looking back, I see that Hawk, Trigger, and Brick heard the news. Their faces are equally as devastated as I’m sure mine is.

“Meet us at the hospital,” I tell them as the ambulance door is closed. I hold tight to Rose’s hand. I have a feeling I won’t let her out of my sight for a long time to come.

# Chapter Twenty-Four

*Rose*

"Baby wake up. The Doctor wants to talk to you."

"Hmm," I open my eyes to a bright room and instantly close them again.

"Thanks, Doc. Try again, baby. The lights are dim."

I open my eyes again, this time to a darker room. Then everything comes rushing back. The fire, Hernández, Princess being shot, being chained up, Bear dead, finally giving up, and then…Bear, saving me.

"She's dead, Bear. I tried to save her. I did whatever I could to protect her. We were almost to the tree line when she was shot." Tears are running down my face and I can't contain the agony as it fights its way out.

"I know, baby. The detectives want to talk to you about everything that happened. But, right now we are going to focus on getting you better, okay?"

I nod my head and look at the doctor.

"How are you feeling Mrs. Allington?"

Allington? I glance over at Bear and see a possessive gleam in his eyes. So, he's the one responsible. I try my best to hide my grin. Allington does sound like the world's most perfect name.

"Well," I tell the doctor, "my head feels heavy and I can't really feel my body."

"There's a reason for both of those," he says. "You have a grade four concussion. That's why your head feels heavy. We will be keeping a close eye on you over the next few days."

"And, why is my whole body numb?" I ask.

"That's because you are on some pretty heavy pain meds, baby."

"Pain medication?"

"What else haven't you told us, doc?" Bear asks.

"Mrs. Allington, you have a patellar fracture in your right knee that will require a cast for about seven weeks. Your left knee is bruised and swollen but will be fine in a couple of weeks."

He's not done. I can tell there's more.

"What else," I manage to whisper.

"You have a Humerus Fracture in your upper right arm. That will need to be in a sling for about four or five weeks. Your left shoulder was dislocated. We've already fixed it, but it will be sore for a little while. Your wrists have some abrasion on them. Just need to keep the bandages and the wounds clean until it's fully healed."

"My knees? Will I be able to walk?" I ask, afraid of the answer.

"With assistance and after we cast your right knee. You can use a cane or crutches to help get around."

"Thank you, doctor," Bear says.

"I hope you get to feeling better soon, Mrs. Allington. Mr. Allington."

The doctor makes a note on his computer before leaving the room.

"I was so worried, Rose. You took about ten years off my life."

"I took all of the years from Princess's life," I say as tears, once again because I'm a freaking baby, fall down my face. "How can you ever forgive me?"

Bear's silent for a while before he speaks again.

"There's nothing to forgive, baby. You didn't do anything wrong. Princess dying was not, in any way, your fault."

"I brought this whole situation into your life, Bear. Into her life. And because of that, her life is over. How can it not be my fault?"

## ****Bear****

***I can't take*** the look of guilt in her eyes anymore. I stand up from where I was sitting beside her bed, and as carefully as I can, I somehow squeeze my body into the bed beside her.

"Listen, I understand what you're saying. I understand what you're thinking." I lean down and kiss away a salty tear, trying not to touch any other part of her body. She bruised all over.

"But, it's simply not true. Hernández was already part of our future before you ran into mine. We were already working on plans to take him down. Losing Princess was a punch in all of our hearts. But, in the end, we got revenge. Maybe not the kind I want, but Hernández is behind bars with his father and every other son of a bitch we could find that was associated with him."

I can see Rose is having a difficult time accepting what I'm saying. But we have all the time in the world for her to feel the truth.

I grab her left hand and slide on the one thing I've kept secret from her. Kissing her beautiful hand, I gently lay it on her stomach...and wait.

And wait...

Her tears have finally stopped and we're laying in her

bed watching tv. I can't help the grin on my face as I gently slide my fingers through her hair.

Any minute now.

It's taken her about an hour before she raises her hand to scratch her face. I see the grimace of pain it causes her, and I get pissed all over again. Of course, that feeling takes a back burner when I see she has finally noticed her surprise.

"What...wow, this is the most beautiful ring. It's for me?"

My Rose is so innocent. I plan to take that innocence for myself and dirty it up.

"Yeah, baby. It's for you. It's your engagement ring."

"My engagement ring? But I don't remember being asked to get married," she tells me with a smirk.

"That's because you weren't asked. Asking would imply you get the chance to say no. You will be my wife, future Mrs. Allington. I will be your husband. That's all there is to it." I leave no room for argument.

"Oh, very well," she agrees with a beautiful smile.

My Rose. My sweet, beautiful Rose.

# Chapter Twenty-Five
## *(four months later)*
## *Bear*

I'm a fucking saint. I've kept my cock away from Rose for about five months. The first month was because she feared this world, feared people, feared me. Then she got hurt by that mother fucker in jail. I told myself that her healing was first and foremost in my mind.

Now, her cast is off, her stint has been removed and she started physical therapy a couple of weeks ago. She can now walk around without her cane. Which is perfect timing, because today, she becomes my wife.

Amara Rosalie Pierce will become mine, completely.

Tonight, I will take Rose Allington into our bed and never let her leave.

****Rose****

***Telling the detectives*** every single detail about the night Roman took me was very hard. I had multiple panic attacks. In the end, my brother actually put a stop to it. Bear wasn't allowed in the room because he kept making threats toward the detectives. I smile at the memory.

It's been four months. Four hard and emotional months. Josh moved about twenty minutes away from our cabin. Turns out, he's married with a baby on the way. I love having him and his wife Michelle around. He's also a prospect for the Infernal Sons. I think he told me he had to be one for a full year before they even considered patching him in.

The clubhouse is in the plans of being rebuilt. I know little beyond the talk of added security. But I do know that everyone is very excited to get it started.

I'm not sure why my mind is having all these random thoughts. I should be focused on the important task before me.

Today, I marry the man I love.

At that thought, I shove all memories to the back of my mind.

"You ready?" Josh asks.

"Absolutely."

"Well, let's go then. I have a sister to give away," he says with a laugh just as the door opens and a woman walks in.

She takes one look at me and bursts into tears. "My Amara. Oh, look how beautiful you are."

I know who she is, Josh has been showing me pictures, but to see her in the flesh is mesmerizing. My mother is beautiful.

"Call me Rose," is what my brain decides should be the very first thing I ever say to my mother.

"Hi Rose," she says through her tears. "I'm Peggy, and this my husband Ryan." She gestures back to the gentleman I hadn't noticed until now.

With a small smile toward her husband, I turn my attention to my mother.

"Hello, mother," I say as I walk forward and wrap her in the tightest of embraces. "You don't have to ask, I understand it now, and I forgive you," I whisper in her ear.

Her crying makes me cry, and now my makeup needs fixing. But I don't care. Today is the best day of my life.

About twenty minutes later, my mother and her husband have gone to find a seat and I've gotten myself under control.

I grab Josh's arm, and he leads me to stand in front of a closed door.

As soon as the doors of the church hall open, I zero in on Bear. He's so handsome standing up there in his white dress shirt, black pants, boots, and his biker vest. I have the strangest urge to release my brother's arm and run toward my soon to be husband.

I held back, but only just.

We reach the end of the aisle and the officiant asks, "Who gives this bride away?"

"I do," Josh answers.

Bear reaches his hand toward me and Josh places my hand into Bears.

"Take care of her man," Josh says to Bear. "Love her as she deserves."

"With everything I am," Bear replies.

Bear pulls me toward his body and whispers in my ear, for only me to hear.

"You are so fucking beautiful, I can't wait to feast on you, baby."

I can feel my blush in full force. Which probably looks crazy against all this white.

I hear people laughing. They may not know what he said, but I'm sure with one quick look at me, they can guess.

"My mother's here."

Is my brain broken? He says the sexiest sentence in all of existence, and I say, my mother's here?

He laughs and says, "I know, I asked her to come. I wanted to surprise you."

"Thank you," I say with my frog voice because I have a giant rock in my throat.

With a smile, Bear grabs my hand and turns us forward.

My groom walks me to the officiant and a handful of minutes later, I become Mrs. Rose Allington.

****Later that night****

*Bear*

***I shut the*** door to our hotel room. Tomorrow morning, we leave for Bora Bora. But tonight, I get to taste my wife.

Finally.

"Wife, you have three minutes to remove any clothing

that you don't want to be torn to shreds."

"What?" she says breathlessly.

"Two minutes and thirty seconds."

She yelps and runs toward the bathroom. One minute later she comes out wearing...nothing.

Holy Fuck!

"Um," she says timidly. "I kind of liked everything and didn't want any of it torn to shreds. I hope this is okay."

"Oh, baby, it's more than okay. It's perfection. Come to your husband, wife. Let me get a good look at what's mine."

I manage to hold still until she's within arm's length, then I grab her and haul her the rest of the way. Gripping the back of her beautiful head, I slam my lips onto hers. The kiss was sweet, sexy and toe-curling all in one.

Grabbing Rose under her delectable ass, I haul her up my body, urging her to wrap her legs around my waist. I walk us to the perfectly made bed and lay her down, holding myself up on my forearms, not wanting to hurt her. All the while, my mouth never leaves hers.

I know this is her first time, so I have to pull in the beast that's trying to break out and go slow. At least for this first round.

Reluctantly, I leave her mouth and spread kisses down her body. Kissing every single scar I pass. I'll never have my wife feeling anything other than absolutely beautiful.

I make it to my destination and gently spread her legs. I see the scars on her thighs for the first time. Put there by her father using dry ice. I feel that anger surge forth before I shove it back and give them gentle kisses.

I take a good look at the pussy that I'm about to devour.

Mmm, where to start?

"Bear, what are you doing?" she asks nervously.

"Hush baby, never interrupt a man who is about to eat like a king."

At her intake of breath, I open my mouth and I feast until her body is shaking with release. Then I eat again until she gives me one more. Licking, sucking every bit of essence she releases.

I stand up and get rid of these pants that are doing a number on my member. Once I release my cock, Rose lets out a little shriek.

"Oh, my word, there's no way," she says.

I throw my head back and laugh. "Oh, yes way, my love. You were made for me, just as I was made for you."

Sliding my cock through her silky folds, I line myself up and gently press forward. She's so fucking tight. It takes everything in me not to come right here like a fucking teenager. Once the tip is inside, I pause to let her adjust and to give me a moment before I embarrass myself in front of my new wife.

"This next part is going to hurt, baby."

"I'm ready, Husband. Make me yours."

Leaning down, I kiss her until I know she isn't thinking about anything else. Then I shove past that thin barrier and claim her as mine.

"Oh, that wasn't so bad," she says about thirty seconds later. "But I need you to move now, Bear. Please, I need..."

"I know what you need, beautiful."

I pull my hips back and push back in slowly. After a few more strokes, Rose lifts her hips silently asking me for more.

I lose all control.

Pulling out until only the tip of my cock rests in her

warm pussy, I slam back in. My hips are out of control as Rose undulates beneath me. I reach between us and rub that perfect little nub wanting my woman to come while I'm inside her.

After a few strokes, she comes apart, squeezing my cock until it feels like it might break right off. I slam myself as far into her as I can and scream my release.

"Fuck," I whisper. All my strength has left, and I collapse beside Rose, pulling her on top of me.

"Wow," she says. "Can we do that again?"

Breathing out a breathless laugh, I say, "You bet your sweet ass we'll be doing that again. Every day for the rest of our lives."

# Epilogue

*(six months later)*

*Rose*

My life is perfect. If I had to go through my entire past again just to live this life, I would do so in a heartbeat. My past was hell, but my future is a dream come true.

Over the past few months, I've been trying to figure out what I want to do with my life. Being a housewife is a beautiful thought. But a greedy one. I've decided to become a social worker and help kids in need. Bear was growly when I told him because it meant time apart while I went to school. But, he's proud of me.

I have a good relationship with my mother. It was awkward at first, but we eventually got past the awkwardness and now I can't picture my life without her in it.

I walk into the kitchen of our cabin to Bear washing dishes. Yep, my husband washes dishes.

"Hey there, handsome," I say breathlessly.

"Baby, is me washing dishes making you wet?" he asks without looking up.

"Maybe," I say.

Throwing his head back, he belts out a laugh.

"Come here, I want to show you what I did today," I tell him.

"Oh, interesting. What did you do today, baby?"

"Here," I hand him a small gift bag.

"What is it?" he asks.

"Open it and see."

Giving me a curious glance, he slowly opens his gift and looks inside.

Without pulling the object out he looks at me with tears in his eyes.

"What do you think, daddy? You have room on your bike for a little someone?"

"You're giving me a baby?" he whispers.

"Yeah honey, we're pregnant. If you pull out your gift, you'll see a picture."

He reaches in the bag and pulls out the infant-sized biker vest and the ultrasound picture I received today. After a few minutes, he places them on the table and picks me up bridal style.

"What are you doing?" I ask with a laugh.

"Going to show my wife how much I love her."

"Forever?" I ask.

"Yes baby, you're my forever."

# The end

Dear Reader,

Thank you so much for reading. Reviews are an author's best friend, so it would mean a great deal to me if you would consider leaving a sentence or two on Amazon or Goodreads.

If you would like to keep up to date with any future releases and giveaways, come join us over at, Carol's Infernal Riders.

# Acknowledgments

Foremost, I want to say thank you to my wonderful man, Jeremy Vanhorn. He's the reason I KNOW insta-love is possible. I also bounced ideas off him for so long before I even started writing. I made him listen to each chapter as I finished to see what he thought. Even though he wasn't the least bit interested, he still sat through each section, patiently, and gave me his opinions and encouragement.

I also want to thank my best friend, Jessi Hensley for taking time out of her daily life to read whatever I sent her. For giving me wonderful advice on how to make the plot or characters better. For helping and encouraging me to reach the finish line.

Thank you to KL Donn for answering my questions and giving me advice, even though she's a very busy bee. And, a huge lovable thanks to my two beautiful boys who lift my spirits up high each and every day.

And last, I want to give credit to a person whom I've never met but has helped me more than he will ever know. After my parents died, ten months apart, I just simply gave up on most things. One of those being writing. Then, one day, I found a YouTuber named, Brandon Farris. After weeks of watching his videos, the way he struggled for a while but never gave up, gave me the final push I needed to finish what I started.

Made in the USA
Columbia, SC
21 February 2020

88253644R00095